THE GOLDEN THREAD

THREAD

A Hidden Falls Romance

THE GOLDEN THREAD

A Hidden Falls Romance

•

Amanda Harte

AVALON BOOKS
NEW YORK

Published by Thomas Bouregy & Co., Inc.
160 Madison Avenue, New York, NY 10016

Library of Congress Cataloging-in-Publication Data

Harte, Amanda.
    The golden thread / Amanda Harte.
        p.   cm. — (The Hidden Falls romance series)
ISBN 978-0-8034-9896-9 (acid-free paper)
I. Title.

PS3515.A79457G65 2008
813'.54—dc22   2007047711

PRINTED IN THE UNITED STATES OF AMERICA
ON ACID-FREE PAPER
BY HADDON CRAFTSMEN, BLOOMSBURG, PENNSYLVANIA

To Deborrah Darroch, whose casual question about a couple minor characters in *The Brass Ring* inspired three new Hidden Falls books. Thanks, Debbie, for that and so much more!

Prologue

*M*ay 1909

"I won't do it."

Eleanor Menger heard the man's quick intake of breath. Slowly, deliberately, he rose from the deep, leather-covered chair and glared down at her. It was not by accident that he'd summoned her to this room, a chamber Eleanor had always thought of as his lair. Here, with the noise of Manhattan traffic muted by thick draperies, he held court, wielding power over all who entered. All except Eleanor.

She remained seated, refusing to blink despite his baleful mien. Though little more than average height, his powerful arms and shoulders, coupled with his pugilistic stance, intimidated most men. As for women . . . Eleanor doubted any would dare to defy him. Aunt Rowena certainly had not. She had been the one who with almost her dying breath had warned Eleanor not to cross him. It was a warning Eleanor refused to heed, especially when the stakes were so high.

Abel Kenton stood in front of her while an unexpected emotion flitted across his face. The fact that Eleanor, a mere female and his supposedly docile ward and niece, had had the temerity to refuse his wishes appeared to have generated as much surprise as anger.

"You're being unreasonable," Uncle Abel said. His voice was as smooth as ever, only the angry glint in his gray eyes betraying his true thoughts. "You know your parents would have . . ."

Eleanor shook her head as she interrupted him. "They would not have wanted me to marry Mr. Warren." She tried not to shudder at the thought of her latest suitor, a widower old enough to be her father but with a gleam in his eyes that said his interest was far from paternal. "Mama always told me I should marry for love."

"Balderdash!" This time her uncle made no attempt to hide his anger, his face darkening until it was only a shade lighter than the somber paneling he'd chosen for the walls. "Marriage is an economic institution."

Aunt Rowena had said something similar when she'd broached the subject of Eleanor's future. Heiresses, she had informed her niece, had responsibilities. Though Eleanor had been tempted to ask her whether those responsibilities included allowing one's husband to squander one's inheritance as Uncle Abel was reported to have done with Aunt Rowena's, she had remained silent. There had been no point in causing her meek-mannered aunt any more pain. Today was different.

Eleanor raised an eyebrow as she looked at her close-to-apoplectic uncle. "Is that the reason Mr. Warren wishes to marry me—for my economic value?"

"Of course not." The reply that came too quickly, accompanied by a furtive glance at the closet door, confirmed Eleanor's fears. Clifford Warren, the current suitor and one of her uncle's closest friends, coveted the substantial estate she would inherit on the earlier of her twenty-fifth birthday or her marriage. As she had suspected, he wasn't interested in Eleanor the person, only Eleanor the heiress.

"Clifford was smitten by your beauty." Once again her uncle's words rang false. Mr. Warren had told Eleanor he preferred dark-haired women and had asked whether she would consider dyeing her reddish-blond curls a more acceptable shade. He had also announced that Missy, as he referred to her, was too thin for his taste— "scrawny" being the adjective he used—and that she would have to put more meat on her bones. Mr. Warren, it appeared, had forgotten any lessons he had once learned about the best way to woo a woman, for his conversation had given Eleanor the impression that she was a calf being fattened for slaughter.

"The answer is the same as it was the last four times," Eleanor said firmly. "I will not marry Mr. Warren."

Her uncle's smile faded, and he took a step closer to her chair. "You must."

She rose, tilting her head slightly in the gesture Mama had once told her was the best way to deal with intractable men. "No, Uncle Abel, that is not something I must do. I will not marry a man I do not love." Surely he should have realized that. In the eight years she'd been his ward, Eleanor had refused a dozen offers of marriage, all for the same reason. When she married— if she married—it would be because a man loved *her*, not the thousands of dollars her father's shrewd investments had provided.

Uncle Abel took another step closer, his stance menacing. "You ungrateful wretch! After all I've done for you, is this how you repay me?"

She shook her head, denying his claim for repayment. "You've given me a place to live. I will grant you that much." Eleanor would not call it a home, for it had not been that, but this gloomy house had provided shelter from the elements, while her aunt's presence had protected Eleanor's reputation. "What I don't understand is why you think I owe you anything, when I've paid my share of expenses." Probably more than her share, but now was not the time for that particular discussion. Eleanor gave her uncle another of the falsely sweet smiles she'd perfected. "If you wish me to leave here, I shall."

His eyes narrowed, then flickered again toward the closet door. "And just how do you propose to live?"

This wasn't the first time Eleanor had considered establishing her own residence, although it was the first time she'd mentioned it to Abel. "My allowance is sufficient for me to live simply." At twenty-four, people would no longer look askance if she lived alone.

Her uncle shook his head, a gloating smile lighting his face. "It won't work that way, Eleanor. I shall withhold your allowance until you agree to marry Clifford."

Though Eleanor's smile faltered, she refused to back down. Uncle Abel was a bully. The only way to deal with him was to refuse to be cowed. "You can threaten all you want," she said as she walked to the door, her actions announcing that this particular meeting was over. "The day I marry Clifford Warren is the day the Hudson River flows north." And that day, Eleanor knew, would never come.

Abel opened the door to the closet, pretending not to notice his friend's scowl. Clifford Warren was tall and lanky with more than a passing resemblance to Abraham Lincoln. But Lincoln had never scowled like this, at least not for formal portraits. Of course, Lincoln probably hadn't had to spend an hour in a dark, cramped closet.

"I thought you told me you could change Missy's mind," Clifford said. "Didn't hear much of that happening. You lost your touch or something?"

"Hardly!" Abel poured his friend a generous serving of whiskey, hoping the fiery brew would sweeten his disposition. He wasn't about to tell Clifford that Eleanor was more obstinate than the proverbial mule, not when he wanted the man to marry that mulelike girl. For what seemed like the hundredth time, Abel rued having the chit in his house. If there hadn't been so much at stake, he'd have tossed her out the day of Rowena's funeral.

"What you heard were empty threats, nothing more. My niece likes baubles. A week or two without a new bonnet and ribbons, and she'll change her tune." Abel shrugged his shoulders, as if the outcome were already determined. "When she does, you and I'll be on easy street. All that money my late and unlamented brother-in-law made will be ours. And then . . ." He let his voice trail off. No point in speaking words that might some day haunt him. Clifford knew what to do.

Chapter One

Was she being followed? Eleanor turned slowly, hoping that if anyone noticed her gesture, they would think she was merely looking at the clock. Less than an hour. If the train was on time, in forty-seven minutes she would leave New York and the life she'd known. Though apprehension mingled with exhilaration, Eleanor managed a small smile. Mama had told her women were as strong as men. This was her chance to prove that. But first she had to board the train.

The station was more crowded than she'd expected, with people milling in every direction. Surely no one would think to look for her here. And even if they did, they would not be searching for a woman of modest means about to take a short journey.

As a conductor announced a departure, a covey of men strode purposefully toward the gate while three women, apparently waiting for a different train, shepherded their children onto one of the wooden benches. A young couple, her hand tucked into the crook of her escort's arm, strolled from one end of the room to the other, their somber expressions making Eleanor suspect only one of them would be boarding a train. Two older men sat on the corner of one of the benches, their heads wreathed by cigar smoke thick enough to practically obscure their features. It was clear they were deep in conversation and cared nothing for their surroundings.

Eleanor felt relief wash through her. It was an ordinary day at Grand Central Station. Ordinary people were going about the business of their ordinary lives. It was only she who was doing something unexpected. And that, she told herself firmly, was the reason she would succeed.

She had spent the last week making careful preparations, taking no one into her confidence. Uncle Abel had seemed pleased when she'd admitted she'd spent her days shopping, reminding her that her purse would not be replenished until she was Clifford Warren's bride. Eleanor doubted he'd have been so pleased if he'd known the nature of her purchases or that she'd found a way to replace her allowance. If she was successful, he would never know.

It should be a few hours before he discovered she was gone. Even then, she doubted he'd realize the departure was permanent. She'd left most of her clothing, stowing only a few treasured possessions in her portmanteau. By the time her uncle realized she wasn't coming back, Eleanor would be miles away from New York, on her way to Hidden Falls and a new life.

She looked around again, trying to make her glances seem casual. No sign of Uncle Abel, the despicable Clifford Warren, or any of her uncle's acquaintances. Of course those men were not here. They had no reason to suspect she'd left Abel's house, and even if they did, they would have no cause to search the train station. When wealthy young women ran away, they did it in style. Only last year Lucy Merriweather had fled, accompanied by her maid and driven by her father's coachman, all because her mother had insisted she wear a most unbecoming shade of green to the Winters' ball. Lucy had been quickly apprehended, but since Mrs. Merriweather had promised that henceforth Lucy could choose her own ball gowns, the prodigal daughter had been more than happy to return home.

Viewing the entire episode as an example of women's lack of common sense, Uncle Abel had spent several dinner hours expounding on the idiocy of Lucy's actions and her mother's spinelessness. At the time, Eleanor had done nothing more than nod politely. Today she breathed a silent prayer that her uncle would remember Lucy and decide that, since his carriage was still safely ensconced in the garage, Eleanor was somewhere inside the house.

As the conductor announced another departure, the two older men rose. Though they walked close enough to Eleanor that she could smell the smoke clinging to their clothing, neither spared her a second glance. Why would they? They were obviously well-to-do. A woman dressed in ill-fitting, second-hand clothing would not attract their attention. Servants, Eleanor knew, were virtually invisible unless they failed at some task. That invisibility was part of her plan.

She straightened her cuffs, trying not to wince as the coarse fabric chafed her skin. Though undoubtedly serviceable, the cotton collar and cuffs were a far cry from the soft linen of her own clothing. *Her former clothing.* Eleanor amended her thought. For the next eleven months, this was what she'd be wearing. For the next eleven months, she would be Eleanor Menger, daughter of a simple New York City shopkeeper, not Eleanor Menger, heiress to a large fortune and Clifford Warren's chosen bride. For the next eleven months, if all went as planned, she would be employed by the Moreland Textile Mills in Hidden Falls. And when those eleven months ended on her twenty-fifth birthday, she would be free. Uncle Abel would have no hold over her. Her inheritance would be hers to do with as she chose. Most important, no one could force her to marry Clifford Warren or anyone else.

"Excuse me, miss. Is this seat taken?"

Eleanor smiled and shook her head at the woman who stood before her. Only a few years older than Eleanor, the woman held a baby in one arm, while the other clasped a toddler's hand. "Here, let me help you." Eleanor picked up the little girl and settled her on the bench next to her.

"Thank you, miss." The woman frowned at her daughter. "She don't normally take to strangers. Truth be told, she don't much like her little brother, either." As the baby began to fuss, the woman turned her attention to him, cooing and calling him "precious."

"Shall I tell you a story?" Eleanor asked the girl. The child shook her head, apparently preferring to glare at her mother and fume over the attention her brother was receiving. Was this an isolated incident, or did the mother favor her son? Eleanor closed her eyes, not liking the direction her thoughts were leading, not wanting to think of how different her life would have been if she'd been a boy. A son, Papa had told her, would have received his inheritance at the age of twenty-one, but women weren't like men. They couldn't handle finances on their own, at least not at such a young age. And so Papa's will had decreed that Eleanor must wait until she was twenty-five or until she had a husband to advise her. Though it had not been a directive, Papa's will had expressed the hope that Uncle Abel would assist Eleanor in the choice of her helpmate. Her uncle had certainly taken that responsibility to heart. She shuddered at the thought of a husband like Clifford Warren. Surely Papa hadn't intended that to be her fate.

She wouldn't think of Clifford Warren, for those thoughts made her stomach churn. Instead, she'd focus her thoughts on happier things. Eleanor looked around, searching for something pleasant. But instead of contented passengers, she saw a young man striding through the waiting room, his clenched fists and the firm line of his mouth telegraphing his anger. Had he not been scowling, the man might have been considered handsome. With auburn hair and a freckled face, he looked like someone born to smile. Today smiles seemed to be forgotten.

Despite herself, Eleanor found her gaze following him, and she started weaving tales, wondering why he was so angry. Had he lost his love? Nonsense. It was only her uncle's insistence on marriage that made Eleanor think others might be unhappy in love. Money troubles? She dismissed the idea as quickly as it appeared. The man's clothing and demeanor told her he had no financial worries. Though she had never met him, Eleanor knew instinctively that he was part of her social class. *Her former social class,* she reminded herself with a sigh. The wealth and privilege she'd once enjoyed were gone, at least temporarily. After today she'd never see the man again. She'd never know what angered him. It didn't matter, of course. What mattered was that she was escaping Uncle Abel's schemes. Tomorrow, if all went well, she would be a mill hand.

How difficult could it be?

The man was impossible. Brad Harrod clenched his fists in a vain effort to dissipate some of his anger as he strode through Grand Central. What he really wanted was to throttle the cause of his anger, but one could hardly do that when the man in question was one's father. Especially when this wasn't the first time they'd had what Brad thought of as The Conversation. He straightened his fingers, clenching them again as he accepted the fact that this was probably not the last iteration, either. Long strides weren't helping, nor were clenched fists. There was no easy cure for this particular problem.

Though it galled him to admit it, Brad had given his father new ammunition. Now, according to Father, he was not only irresponsible, but he also lacked the ability to win a woman's love. As if Brad were to blame for the fact that Jane Moreland loved the town's bad boy! Jane's marriage had utterly no bearing on Brad's ability to run the railroad. Unfortunately, Father didn't see it that way, and he probably never would.

Brad gave the waiting room a quick glance. Thank goodness there was no one he recognized. He wasn't in the mood to talk to anyone, not until he calmed down a bit. Maybe in a decade or so. Appeased by what he had seen—or, more precisely, what he had not seen—he looked around again, this time assessing the passengers, trying to guess their destinations. It was a pastime he'd indulged in for as long as he could recall. How many were going to Hidden Falls and, in doing so, adding to the Harrod Railroad's profits?

His glance landed on two women sharing a bench. The older cradled an infant in her arms, while the younger appeared to be attempting to entertain a small girl. Her daughter? Brad didn't think so. The girl bore a strong resemblance to the older, dark-haired woman. Was the woman with the strawberry-blond hair a relative, he wondered, or simply a friend traveling with the others? His eyes narrowed slightly as he watched the blond glance around the station. Perhaps it was his imagination, but her looks seemed furtive. Intrigued as his overactive imagination began to postulate reasons, Brad studied her more carefully. Her clothing was ordinary, certainly not the kind of clothing his mother or Jane Moreland had ever worn. Her hairstyle was less elaborate than his mother's or Jane's. And yet there was something almost regal about the tilt of her head. Odd.

As Brad strode past the women, he realized that his hands were no longer clenched. If it hadn't been totally inappropriate, he would have thanked the mysterious blond for giving him a reprieve—even if it was only a brief one—from his anger.

"Good afternoon, Mr. Harrod," the conductor said as Brad climbed into the train.

"Good afternoon, James. It doesn't look like we have a full train today." Father would grouse about that and somehow find a way to blame Brad for the disappointing ticket sales.

The conductor shook his head, contradicting Brad. "Not a lot of passengers, but there are three cars of cotton bound for the mills. A good load."

Nodding, Brad entered the first class car. Though he normally traveled in the Harrods' private rail car, he'd left that for Father with the unspoken but fervent hope that his parent would remain in New York City for several days. That would give them both a chance to let their tempers cool.

Mindful of his responsibility as heir apparent to the railroad, Brad greeted the other passengers before settling into a seat. Father was wrong—flat out wrong—when he said Brad didn't care about the railroad and wasn't ready to assume any responsibilities. He cared. He cared more than he wanted to admit. He cared that Father wouldn't listen to his ideas for improving profits. He cared that he had been given not even the slightest responsibility for the running of the railroad. Mostly, he cared that his father did not trust him.

When they'd been students, Brad and his best friends, Anthony and Charles, had believed what they wanted most in life was a life of leisure. At the time the trio, whom classmates had dubbed "The ABCs" because of their first names, had known it was an unrealistic expectation. Charles was already deeply involved in running Moreland Mills with his father, and Anthony had taken on tutoring assignments in preparation for becoming a professor. Only Brad had led a carefree life. The others had claimed to envy him, laughing when he said they were the lucky ones. Their lives had purpose; his did not. A carefree life, Brad could now attest, was boring. And so was this ride.

He rose and walked to the second-class car. He might as well greet those passengers. The car had more passengers than first class but was still close to empty. While it had space for forty, Brad counted fewer than a dozen riders. A family with three children occupied two seats, and four men—farmers, Brad guessed—appeared engrossed in a discussion of crop prices.

Alone in the back of the car sat a solitary woman, her face hidden by a newspaper.

"Good afternoon, ma'am," Brad said when he reached her seat. "I trust you're enjoying the ride."

She lowered the paper, and as she did, Brad's eyes widened. This was the strawberry blond who had provided such a welcome distraction in the waiting room. He had failed at his game of guessing destinations, although—in his defense—she had been sitting so far from the Hidden Falls gate that he hadn't realized she would be one of the passengers on his train.

"It's quite pleasant," the woman said. Her voice was more cultured than he would have expected, its tone melodious. Though she kept her expression impassive other than that first startled look, which made him think she'd recognized him, something about her words told him she was lying, and for the first time Brad studied the seats where the majority of Harrod Railroad's passengers rode. Little more than wooden benches, they clearly lacked the padding the first-class passengers enjoyed. He doubted anyone would describe the ride as pleasant, but perhaps she somehow knew that he was a Harrod and didn't want to antagonize him.

Brad stood for a moment, looking down at her. This woman bore no resemblance to Jane. Her eyes were green, like his, not blue like Jane's. Her features were a bit more delicate than Jane's, her hair brighter than Jane's golden blond, and she appeared to be an inch or two shorter than the woman he had once courted. Other than the fact that they were both young women, there were no similarities. But still something reminded him of Jane. Perhaps it was the innate dignity he'd observed in the waiting room. And so, though he had no reason to tarry, Brad found himself loath to return to his well-padded seat in the other car.

"Are you going to Hidden Falls?" he asked, wanting to prolong the conversation. Though that was the terminus of the rail, there were several stops between New York and Brad's hometown.

"Yes, I am." Her voice, while still polite, bore a hint of dismissal, and that intrigued Brad as much as her regal air. Women never dismissed Brad Harrod, not if they knew who he was. His father's fortune guaranteed that.

"I don't believe I've seen you there." The truth was, Brad knew he'd never seen her. This was not a woman whose face he would have forgotten.

She raised one eyebrow in a gesture Brad had seen his mother use on numerous occasions when she wanted to put a gentleman in his place. "This will be my first visit," the woman said, inclining her head ever so slightly. "And now if you'll excuse me, sir . . ." Without waiting for his reaction, she picked up the newspaper. There was no doubt about it. He had been dismissed.

"Sorry to have bothered you, ma'am." A mirthless chuckle escaped his lips as he left the car. Once again he'd proven his father correct. Not only had he been unable to convince Jane Moreland to marry him, but he even couldn't get this woman to carry on a brief conversation with him. Brad Harrod was less interesting than a day-old newspaper. How humiliating!

He frowned as he took his seat. What did people see in newspapers, anyway? His mother devoured the society pages, taking great delight in the comings and goings of her friends in New York and Philadelphia. His father perused the business section, claiming important trends were there, if only the wise man knew where to look. But other than those few pages, the papers printed nothing but bad news. Why would anyone voluntarily spend time reading that?

On the opposite side of the aisle, Harold Cutler laid down his paper, his face marred by an uncharacteristic frown.

"May I borrow your paper?" Brad asked.

"You can keep it." Mr. Cutler practically tossed the newspaper at him. "I don't know why I spend good money on rags like that. It makes a man downright depressed to read them."

Though his neighbor was obviously perturbed, Brad's spirits rose. He wasn't alone in his opinion of modern journalism. He nodded, encouraging Mr. Cutler to continue.

"If the world is as bad as that paper says, I can't imagine why anyone would want to live in it."

Brad nodded again. "I couldn't have said it better myself." Unlike his parents, he did not believe any value to be found on the society or business pages mitigated the deplorable reporting that constituted the majority of the news. Brad opened the paper, frowning at the headlines. "You'd think someone could report some good news."

The look Mr. Cutler gave Brad said he was naïve. "Publishers need to make a profit, and good news doesn't sell papers."

"That's a shame, isn't it?"

For the next hour, Brad read the paper, refusing to skip even the most mundane of articles, and as he read, his frown deepened. It wasn't simply that the paper reported bad news. That was deplorable in itself, but what was worse was how it was done. With headlines that emphasized the sensational aspect of each article and lurid descriptions of every crime, no matter how petty, the reader had no respite from negativism. Even a report of a lost dog had been turned into a jeremiad about the perils of owning an animal, when it could have been a rallying cry to enlist the townspeople's aid in finding a little boy's pet.

When he'd read the last inch of print, Brad settled back in his seat and closed his eyes. Newspapers were important. They had been for centuries, providing a way of informing the masses. They were powerful tools, shaping opinion, helping expose criminal activities, promoting philanthropic organizations. When had they changed into this? Brad glared at the paper he'd read so carefully. He wouldn't dismiss the realities of needing to make a profit. Living with Father had impressed on him the importance of profit and loss statements and the need for the former to outweigh the latter. Profits were necessary if a newspaper or a railroad were to continue in existence, but surely there was a better way to inform people of daily events. Surely there was an alternative to sensationalism, something that would sell papers without depressing the readers. The question was, what was it?

Brad closed his eyes again, seeking an answer. Unbidden, the image of the woman in the second-class car rose before him. She'd attracted his attention the moment he'd first spotted her in the waiting room, and that was unusual. Though he'd played his "guess the destination" game for years, this was the first time he had noticed—really noticed—one of the passengers. Why? What was different about this woman? She was beautiful, but so were many women. Something else had intrigued him. Brad's thoughts whirled. It wasn't her clothing or the fact that she traveled alone. What was the difference? He recalled the confident tilt of her head and the polite but cool smile. Though obviously a member of the working class, the strawberry blond possessed an instinctive dignity that rivaled even his mother's. Dignity. Brad grinned. That was the answer.

Chapter Two

She had arrived. With the exception of the one interruption, the train trip had been uneventful, bringing her to Hidden Falls precisely on schedule. And now, mere minutes later, she was approaching her destination. Inside her gloves, her hands grew moist with apprehension. Had she made the right decision? Would she be able to do this?

"This be it." The driver pointed as he slowed the wagon. As much to calm her nerves as from curiosity, Eleanor looked at the building destined to be her home for close to a year. Made of red brick, it was more attractive than she'd expected. Oh, there were none of the stately white columns and large windows that had characterized her parents' house, but the square building had pleasing proportions, with gables softening the roof line. Though it could have benefited from window boxes and flowers planted next to the foundation, Eleanor reminded herself that this was not a private residence but rather a commercial boardinghouse. The residents were likely more concerned with cleanliness and comfortable mattresses than exterior beautification. That was what would matter to her too.

"You must be Eleanor." A tall, thin woman answered Eleanor's knock and ushered her inside. "I'm Mrs. Weld."

Eleanor took an involuntary step backward, unsure which had surprised her more: the fact that Mrs. Weld had addressed her by her first name or the appraising look the older woman was giving her. *Don't be a ninny,* Eleanor told herself firmly. *You're not "Miss Menger" here. You're a mill worker.* Apparently mill hands were, like the servants in her parents' home, referred to by their first names. And the woman's appraisal was nothing more than normal curiosity. It was only silly, silly Eleanor who feared that Mrs. Weld could see behind the surface and would realize how out of place she was.

There was no reason to fear this woman's gaze any more than she should have been alarmed by the man who'd spoken to her on the train. At the time Eleanor had been startled, seeing the Angry Man, as she'd named him, on the same train. Surprise had turned to an irrational concern that he might be working for Uncle Abel, and that had made her more curt than normal. It was only after he left and she overheard other passengers referring to him as Mr. Harrod that Eleanor realized how groundless her worries had been. As part of the family that owned the railroad, he was simply being courteous, welcoming riders. Her behavior, on the other hand, had bordered on rude, and that filled Eleanor with chagrin. In the future, she'd be careful not to let fears override common sense and the courtesy Mama had taught her.

"Come in, Eleanor." The woman's voice brought her back to the present, its warmth dispelling her doubts. "I imagine you'd like a cup of tea after your journey." Mrs. Weld led the way to the kitchen and gestured toward a small table. In less time than the servants at home would have taken to simply measure the tea, Mrs. Weld had brought out a teapot, poured boiling water, retrieved a cup and saucer, and placed them in front of Eleanor, all without seeming to rush. Watching this model of efficiency, Eleanor began to relax.

"The other girls will be arriving in a few minutes," the housemother said as she turned back to the stove. "I'd sit and visit with you, but I need to have their food ready."

As she sipped her tea, Eleanor stared in amazement at the stove where cauldron-sized pots were simmering. She had never seen so much food being prepared at one time. Surely a few girls could not consume even a fraction of it.

One second, the house was silent, save for the bubbling of the stew and the sound of Mrs. Weld's footsteps. The next an explosion of noise filled it. Never before had Eleanor heard so many voices speaking so loudly. When she had attended the theater, the voices had been modulated. This was different. It sounded as if a hundred women were shouting at each other, all at the same time. Was anyone listening? Instinctively, Eleanor covered her ears.

Mrs. Weld chuckled. "You'll get used to it. The girls tell me mealtime conversation is peaceful compared to the mill."

This was mealtime conversation? Perhaps it was, although not the type Eleanor was accustomed to. This reminded her of the tigers at the zoo as feeding time approached. The large cats had roared when they smelled fresh meat. Was that what these women were doing? And how many were there? When she'd first looked at the building, Eleanor had assumed it held fifteen to twenty residents. Surely even twenty young women could not make this much noise.

As two women whose strong resemblance told Eleanor they were sisters entered the kitchen, Mrs. Weld turned toward her. "Eleanor, these are Virginia and Deborah Sempert. They'll show you around."

"I'm Virginia," the taller of the two said. Eleanor noted with relief that her own clothing was similar to the sisters'. At least her appearance would not cause undue speculation. "Has Mrs. Weld taken you to our room?" Virginia continued.

Our room? It sounded as if Eleanor would be sharing a chamber with the two sisters. "Not yet," she said as calmly as she could, although she had never shared a room, not even when her favorite cousin had come to visit. She should have realized that accommodations here would be substantially different from her home, even from Uncle Abel's house. After all, none of her parents' or her uncle's servants had private rooms. Mill workers might not be domestic help, but they belonged to the same social class. Like the coarse fabric of her garments, limited privacy would be part of Eleanor's new life. Freedom, she told herself, had its price.

As Virginia opened the door, Mrs. Weld shook her head. "There's no time now. Dinner will be ready in two minutes."

"You'll be at our table," Deborah told Eleanor. Though there was no denying the sisters' physical similarities, there were also differences. An inch shorter and perhaps a year or two younger than her sister, Deborah's hair was several shades darker than Virginia's, her eyes chocolate brown while Virginia's were hazel. And while no one would call her heavy, Deborah had generous curves in contrast to Virginia's slender form.

Deborah led the way into the dining room, which was, Eleanor realized, the source of the din. Three long tables, each accommodating twelve diners, filled the room. Two oil paintings hung on the wall, and a pair of brass candlesticks graced one corner of the mantel. It was an ordinary room, except for the roar of what seemed like a hundred different conversations. Eleanor had never realized that three dozen women could be so loud.

As she sank into one of the empty chairs, Deborah introduced Eleanor to the other women at their table.

"You'll get used to the noise," one of the women said with a reassuring smile. Eleanor wasn't so certain.

Though she'd traveled less than two hundred miles from home, she felt as if she were in a whole new world.

As Mrs. Weld continued to place plates laden with food on the table, Eleanor shook her head. "I've never seen so much food," she confessed. In addition to the hearty beef stew she had seen cooking, her plate was laden with fried potatoes and pancakes covered with slices of stewed apples. A second plate held thick slices of brown bread and cheese, while a third had chunks of blueberry cake and two generous portions of Indian pudding topped with cream. All of that, it appeared, would be washed down with either coffee or water.

"Didn't you eat much on the farm?" Virginia asked. Like the other women at the table, she appeared to be enjoying both the quantity and the quality of the food. It was delicious, Eleanor had to admit. She was hungrier than she'd realized. The savory food combined with the sudden silence as the residents devoted themselves to eating stimulated her appetite.

"I didn't live on a farm," Eleanor said. When she'd learned that most of the mill hands had rural backgrounds, Eleanor had felt a moment of panic. There was no way she could sustain the pretense of being a farmer's daughter. Instead, she'd decided not to hide her urban roots. "Papa was a shopkeeper," she said, beginning the story she'd invented. That wasn't a lie; it simply wasn't the whole truth. Her father had once owned a haberdashery, but when he discovered that he had a knack for picking good investments, he sold the shop and devoted his time to backing promising companies.

"That explains your lack of appetite," Virginia said with a knowing nod. "You'll soon discover you need every bit of what Mrs. Weld serves just to get through the day."

"Think of it as fuel," Deborah offered as she reached for her dessert plate. "You need it to keep your engine running."

Eleanor smiled, relieved that attention had been diverted from her fictional former life. "That's the first time I've heard the human body described that way."

"You'll find there are a lot of firsts here."

Eleanor couldn't help agreeing with Virginia's statement. She only hoped that most of them proved to be pleasant. The highest hurdles, she knew, remained. Though she'd tried and failed to imagine what work in a textile mill would be like, the fact that so much food—fuel, according to Deborah—was needed did not reassure Eleanor. Had she made a mistake, thinking she could do this?

Oblivious to Eleanor's concerns, Virginia continued. "This is the first time Deborah and I have been away from the farm."

"But we're going back," her sister said as she finished her Indian pudding, apparently savoring the molasses-and-cornmeal concoction.

"Deborah's saving her money so she can marry one of our neighbors." In the corner, a tall clock chimed the half hour, the sound causing several of the women to take larger bites of their food, hurrying to finish their meals as if they feared being late for an engagement.

"Deborah and Franklin have been sweet on each other for years," Virginia said.

A faint blush stained Deborah's cheeks. "Eleanor doesn't want to hear about us." She turned to Eleanor. "Tell us why you came here. Are you saving money for a dowry?"

Quite the contrary. Eleanor wondered what the Sempert sisters would say if they knew just how extensive her dowry was and that she had come to Hidden Falls to avoid giving that dowry to Clifford Warren. Those were things no one needed to know, and so she said only, "I have no plans to marry anytime soon." Deborah's sympathetic look made her add, "I haven't found the right man."

As she pronounced the words, the image of the man who'd spoken to her on the train flitted through Eleanor's brain. Absurd! She'd seen Mr. Harrod twice and doubted she would see him again. Though Hidden Falls was a small town, their paths were unlikely to cross, for the owner of the railroad would not spend time near the mill or in the company of mill hands. It wasn't as if he'd singled her out for attention. He had been polite, trying to strike up a conversation on the train, nothing more. Once they reached Hidden Falls, they'd gone in different directions.

Besides, even if Eleanor did encounter him, there was no reason to be thinking of Mr. Harrod and marriage in the same sentence. He wouldn't be interested in a mill worker, and she wasn't interested in marriage. Hadn't she spent the last few years declaring exactly that to Uncle Abel and the men who'd tried to win her hand?

Though she had no intention of admitting the direction her thoughts had taken, both sisters appeared to be waiting for additional explanations, and so Eleanor said softly, "My parents died and . . ." She dropped her gaze as she let her words trail off.

"Say no more." Virginia touched her hand in sympathy. "We didn't mean to pry. It's just that we'll be sharing a room and we hope we can be friends."

The meal was over, and the other women had started to leave the dining room. "Eleanor probably wants to see our room. I can show her." Deborah nodded at her sister. "I know you want to go to the lending library."

As she led the way up the stairs, Deborah said, "My sister loves to read."

"And you don't?" They had climbed two steep flights of stairs, leaving Eleanor a bit breathless.

"Books are fine, but I prefer songs. I could sing all day if anyone would listen."

As they reached the top of the third flight, Deborah opened a door. "Here it is. I hope you don't mind a trundle bed."

Eleanor stood in the doorway, trying not to let her shock show. The room she was expected to share with two other women was less than half the size of her bedchamber at home. A double bed and a trundle positioned dangerously close to the sloped ceiling occupied most of the floor space. Since there was no other furniture save a small table with a ewer and washbasin, clothing hung from pegs on the wall rather than being carefully folded in drawers or placed on hangers in a sweetly-scented armoire. Although the room boasted one of the gables Eleanor had admired only an hour earlier, little light streamed through the glass. Instead, a gaslight on one wall provided basic illumination. How did one read under these conditions? Like Virginia, Eleanor enjoyed a good book.

"We're fortunate." Deborah gestured around the room. "This may be the smallest room, but there are only three of us sharing it. The other rooms all have three beds each—six girls to a room."

Six in one room. Eleanor's mind reeled at the thought. *It's only eleven months*, she reminded herself. *You can do anything for eleven months.* Even if she had to share a bedchamber with sixty women, it would be better than the alternative. At least she was not living with Clifford Warren.

Far earlier than she'd ever risen, the first bell of the day wakened her. Eleanor followed the sisters' lead and before she was fully awake, she'd dressed, eaten as much as she could of the enormous breakfast that Mrs. Weld served, and was now on her way to the mill. The crowd of women who hurried toward the five-story red-brick building reminded Eleanor of a herd of sheep. There was one difference, though. While sheep bleated, the women were, for the most part, silent. Perhaps they, like Eleanor, were half asleep.

"I'll introduce you to Mr. Greeley," Virginia said as

they climbed yet another flight of stairs. "He's our overseer, and he has to approve all the new girls." Eleanor's dismay must have shown, for Virginia added, "Don't worry. It's a formality now that Mrs. Weld vouched for you."

A light went off in Eleanor's brain. That was why Mrs. Weld had watched her so carefully when she'd arrived. She'd been trying to determine whether Eleanor would make a good mill hand. Moreland Mills, like its competitors, prided itself on hiring only honest, hard-working women.

"You'll be working with me for the first few months." Though Eleanor was out of breath by the time they reached the fifth floor, Virginia seemed not at all winded.

"My sister's the best teacher," Deborah explained. "That's why Mr. Greeley assigns most of the apprentices to her." The advertisement that had led Eleanor to Moreland Mills had promised "sufficient instruction" as well as "ample, nutritious fare." When she'd read those words, she had pictured a classroom. How naïve of her. Weaving was not like Greek or Latin. One did not learn a practical skill like operating a loom by reading a book or listening to a professor expound on the technique. One learned by doing.

"I hope I can do it," she said, voicing the fear that had hounded her from the moment she'd decided to leave New York.

"Of course you can."

Half an hour later, Eleanor was not so certain. When she'd first entered the weaving room, she was sure she'd been transported to one of Dante's circles of hell, a place where one could neither breathe nor hear. How often had she complained that New York City was hot and humid during the summer months? She'd complain no more, for the discomfort of the city could not compare to this. Here the air was so thick with moisture that Eleanor found herself trying not to breathe, lest her lungs fill with water and choke her.

"You'll get used to it," Virginia said, giving Eleanor's hand a reassuring pat when she gasped at the sight of two women wielding huge sprayers, each shooting gallons of mist into the air. "We need the water in the air to keep the threads from breaking. See how the plants like it." As Eleanor followed the direction of Virginia's glance, she saw windowsills lined with green plants, their lush foliage corroborating Virginia's statement. This was obviously an atmosphere where plants and cotton thrived and mill hands learned to survive.

The heat and humidity, oppressive as they were, paled compared to the noise assailing Eleanor's ears. A hundred looms, the shuttles moving faster than she had imagined possible, thumped, creating a cacophony louder than an approaching locomotive and more piercing than the screech of a subway car shuddering to a stop. How did anyone manage to work here, day after day? Women are strong, Mama had said. These women certainly were. It remained to be seen whether Eleanor possessed even a modicum of their strength and tenacity.

Within minutes, her head began to throb and she was

convinced her hearing was permanently damaged. Though Virginia personified patience, repeating her instructions dozens of times, Eleanor doubted she'd ever have the dexterity to thread a shuttle or the skill to knot broken warp. This was like nothing she'd ever learned. She could paint a watercolor, play the pianoforte, and tat a delicate edging, but this—this was far more difficult. How could anyone learn anything in these conditions? Why, simply understanding instructions was almost impossible. While the other mill hands used hand gestures to communicate, that was a language Eleanor did not know. She had to hear what Virginia was saying, and so she learned that bending her head, placing her ear close to Virginia's mouth, was the only way she could hope to hear her teacher's instructions.

When the dinner bell sounded and the looms fell silent, Eleanor could still hear ringing in her ears. "How do you survive?" she asked Virginia as they made their way down the stairs, Eleanor gripping the railing to support legs that felt as limp as unwoven cotton.

"It gets easier," Virginia assured her.

Deborah, who'd joined them, chuckled. "I told you you'd need fuel. Eat everything on your plate now." And, though a day ago she would have thought it impossible, Eleanor did.

When the final bell of the day rang and the women returned to the boardinghouse for supper, Eleanor discovered her feet were so swollen she could barely walk. "I never guessed it was so difficult."

"You're doing well." Virginia continued the encouragement she'd given Eleanor all day. "You're learning quickly."

"I only wish that were true." What she really wished, Eleanor realized as she collapsed on her bed after supper, was that this whole charade wasn't necessary. But it was, unless she wanted to marry Clifford Warren. Suddenly, a ferocious headache and swollen feet didn't seem like too high a price to pay, not when freedom was at stake.

"So, what do you think?" Brad feigned nonchalance, as if his friend's response were of little importance. The truth was, it mattered more than anything Brad could remember. For the first time, he understood the expression "all fired up," for that was how he felt, as if someone had lit a fire deep inside him. His thoughts boiled faster than the steam engines that powered his father's locomotives, filling him with seemingly boundless energy and a determination to turn his dream into reality. He'd slept little last night. Instead, he'd spent the hours scribbling notes, trying to anticipate each step he'd have to take. Now that it was morning and what Mother would call a civilized hour, he'd come to the mill, needing to confide in his best friend. What would Charles think?

At first Charles Moreland said nothing, merely leaned back in his chair. It was, Brad suspected, a technique designed to make him squirm, probably something Charles had learned from his father. What Brad had learned from his own father was the importance of patience. Right now that patience was being tried.

As if he realized Brad had reached his limit, Charles spoke, his words laced with mirth. "I'm still trying to recover from the shock," he announced. "Brad Harrod, gainfully employed. Has the earth stopped revolving on its axis?" Charles propped his feet on his desk, the picture of an indolent man. "I can't wait to tell Anthony about this."

It was not the response Brad had expected and certainly not the one he'd wanted. "You and Anthony can laugh all you want," he said with more than a hint of asperity. This was not a laughing matter, at least not to him. "Don't forget that I'm the only one of us who's kept the pact."

"What pact?" Brad wasn't sure how Charles managed to sound so innocent.

"You two conveniently forgot that we all vowed not to marry before our thirtieth birthdays." While they'd still been in college together, the ABCs had declared they would not follow in their parents' footsteps. They'd never get tied down to ordinary lives, lives that included marriage and children, at least until they'd had a chance to savor independence for another decade. "Anthony's been wed for more than a year and look at you, Charles. You're married and already expecting your first child." He gave his friend an accusing look. "Didn't our college friendship mean anything to you?"

Charles shrugged. "Of course it did, but priorities change. You'll understand when you fall in love."

"I was . . ."

Without letting him complete the sentence, Charles shook his head. "I don't think so. You may have fancied yourself in love with my sister, but I never thought you and she were meant to be together."

"Sound the trumpets." Brad could match Charles for sarcasm. "This must be the first time you and Jane have agreed." It was also the first time Charles had admitted that he'd had doubts about Brad's one-time desire to marry Jane. While he'd been courting her, Charles had supported him.

"As much as it pains me to admit it," Charles said, "my sister is happy with Matt. And one day, my friend, you will be happy with someone else. Charles the oracle has spoken. Now, tell me, what made you decide you should found Hidden Falls' first newspaper?"

Brad hesitated for a second. Should he tell Charles the truth? Why not? "A woman."

The look of pure shock on Charles's face was priceless. "I was right," Brad's friend said when he'd recovered his composure. "You weren't pining for Jane after all."

"Sorry to disappoint you, but there was nothing romantic about this woman." Although she did have one of the most beautiful faces he'd seen, and those green eyes shone more than his mother's emerald ring. But there was no reason—absolutely no reason—to mention that to Charles. "It was simple, really. There was this woman riding the train, and she acted as if the paper she was reading was the most fascinating thing on earth."

Charles nodded slowly. "And since she wasn't fascinated by you personally, you wanted to do the next best thing and be the man responsible for the paper that created that fascination."

Was that the reason? Brad hadn't considered the possibility that he'd been reacting to the woman's dismissal. How shallow would that make him, if his decision was based on pique? But it hadn't been. The woman's preoccupation with the written word had simply been the match that lit the fire. The newspaper was a good idea. At least he thought it was. Charles still hadn't weighed in with his opinion.

"I want to give everyone in Hidden Falls an alternative to the gloom-sayers," Brad explained. "So tell me, and be honest. What do you think of the idea?"

This time there was no hesitation, no anxiety-producing delay in answering. "It's a capital one." Charles accompanied his words with a decisive nod. "If anyone can make a success of it, it's you."

Slowly Brad exhaled, feeling the tension drain from him along with his breath. "Thanks, Charles. Your opinion means a lot to me."

Charles looked down at his desk, as if uncomfortable with the direction the conversation had taken. "Have you picked a location for the office and printing press?" he asked.

"I haven't decided. I looked at some land at the western end of Mill Street, not too far from your sister's nursery. I'd have to construct a building, of course, but that shouldn't take more than a few months."

Charles twirled a pen between his fingers, then rose and walked to the window. "Would you consider becoming my tenant?" He pointed toward a one-story brick building just east of the mill. "Now that your trains are running more frequently, I don't need to stock inventory, so that building is virtually empty. You could turn it into a printing shop. The rent won't be too exorbitant."

Brad's mind began to whirl with the possibilities. The location Charles had proposed was better than the one he'd selected, and the fact that the building already existed meant that he'd be able to get the paper started far more quickly than he'd anticipated.

"Are you sure, Charles?"

"Absolutely. I'll even be one of your first advertisers."

"You're a real friend."

A wry smile lit Charles's face. "Even if I did renege on our pact?"

"Even if."

Despite the fact that his voice had once caused Charles's dogs to howl in pain, Brad was singing aloud as he drove home. No one was close enough to hear him, and no matter how toneless his singing was, it felt right to be singing, just as the decisions he'd made felt right. The sense of aimless wandering that had plagued him for so long was gone. Now he knew what he wanted. Now that he'd found a direction for his life, he was anxious to tell his parents about it.

Mother would be happy, but, then again, everything he

did seemed to please her. Though Father had always been the difficult one, the disapproving parent, that would change tonight. After tonight Father could no longer claim that Brad was irresponsible, for his son was about to become an entrepreneur. As soon as the attorney could complete the paperwork, Brad would own a business, and soon after that he'd hire his first employees.

Those were heady thoughts, cause for yet another chorus of "She'll Be Comin' Round the Mountain." As he parked the Model T in front of his parents' house, Brad was grinning, picturing the strawberry blond driving six white horses. She'd given him the inspiration he'd needed. Thanks to her, he had his plan. He had Charles's approval and soon he'd have his parents'. What more could a man want?

"The roast was delicious, Mother. Thank you for ordering it." At last the meal was coming to an end. When Brad had decided to save his announcement for dessert, he'd forgotten how long some meals seemed to take. Without being rude, he could not pull out his watch, but surely at least three hours had passed since they'd entered the dining room. Now, finally, the time had come.

His mother smiled in response to the compliment. "When you said you had something important to tell us, I wanted to make dinner special."

Father raised an eyebrow. "An announcement? What sort of announcement would that be?"

The faint condescension in his father's tone made Brad's hackles rise. Reminding himself that would change once he'd heard the news, Brad inhaled deeply in an attempt to control his temper. Now was not the time to argue. Instead, he said calmly, "I thought about what you said and realized I was wasting my life, waiting for you to let me play a role at the railroad."

His father's lips thinned with disapproval. "You'll have a role as soon as you're ready. I've seen no signs of that so far."

Flinching, Brad realized he'd made a mistake. This was not going the way he'd expected. Perhaps he should not have mentioned the railroad.

Always the peacemaker, his mother laid a hand on her husband's arm. "Please, Jacob, let Brad continue."

He said nothing while the butler placed dessert plates in front of them. There was no point in fueling speculation. The fact that Mother had ordered special foods, including the floating island that was Father's favorite dessert, had probably already provoked a spate of questions in the kitchen. It was only when the door was once more closed that Brad continued, "I'm going to start my own business." He felt as if he'd thrown down a gauntlet. To his surprise, his father said nothing, merely raised his eyebrow again in a gesture meant to be intimidating. "I'm going to publish a newspaper, the *Hidden Falls Herald*."

For a moment the room was silent. Though Mother continued to smile, the smile faded ever so slightly when she looked at her husband. His face had reddened, and his lips twisted in a scowl. Even more ominously, he had pushed the dessert plate away. In Brad's memory, Father had never failed to eat every bite of floating island.

"That is the most ridiculous scheme I've ever heard," his father said, his voice harsh with condemnation. "What will you find to report? Who will buy it? And—most important—who would pay to advertise in it?" He fired the questions with the force of a cannonball.

Brad tried not to wince at his father's displeasure. Why had he thought tonight would be different from all the other times he'd ventured an idea, only to have it shot down? Just because he was excited and Charles enthusiastic didn't mean Father would agree. He should have realized that. Brad fixed his gaze on the still-life painting that had graced the far wall for as long as he could remember. He cared not a whit for the bowl of fruit it portrayed, but staring at apples and pears was preferable to seeing his father's displeasure.

It would be simple to do what he'd done so many times before and walk away. Perhaps that's what he should do, but tonight there was more at stake than ever before. Tonight it was his future he was discussing.

Slowly and deliberately, Brad explained his vision, hoping that once he'd heard it, Father would understand. "I'll report local news, of course. That's what concerns people most. Besides, they like seeing their names in print. But there'll be national and international news too."

With a resigned sigh, Father reached for his dessert plate and took a spoonful of the custard. "There's no need for national news," he said when he'd nodded his approval of the sweet. "People can get that information from the big city papers."

"No, they can't." In the past, Brad might have remained silent, seething inwardly as his father tried to destroy his dreams. He would not do that again. "No one reports news the way I plan to."

A look of sheer incredulity met his words. "And what way would that be?" His father's voice dripped with sarcasm. "Have you invented some new language?"

Brad took a small bite of the dessert as he tried to control his frustration. Why wouldn't Father listen? Why did he persist in considering Brad a child, unable to form a coherent thought? "You might call it that," he said as calmly as he could. "The *Herald* will use the language of optimism. I see no reason why people should be depressed or disgusted by what they read."

"It's ridiculous. Totally impractical." Father didn't bother to hide his anger. "You'll fail at this as you have at everything else you've tried." Once again pushing his dessert aside, he turned to his wife. "I tell you, Mae, if the boy didn't look like me, I'd wonder if he were someone else's son."

Mother blanched, then gave Brad a beseeching look. For years, she had counseled Brad not to antagonize his father, and he'd listened, sometimes literally biting his tongue rather than responding with anger. He could do that no longer.

"You're wrong, Father." To Brad's relief, his voice was steady, his words firm. The fact that he felt as if he'd been pummeled was not apparent in his tone. "I am not a failure." He took a deep breath, letting the words linger in the air before he continued. It was time his parents understood how he felt. It was time they realized he was not a child. "How could I fail when you haven't given me a chance to fail . . . or to succeed? I'm going to do this. I'm going to create the *Herald,* and I will not fail."

If his father heard the accusation in Brad's words, he gave no sign. "You're wasting your time and money on this harebrained scheme," he said, his voice colder than Brad could remember it. "There is no need for a newspaper in Hidden Falls. You'll soon discover that, and when you fail—as you surely will—I'll be the laughingstock of the town. I don't know how your mother and I will be able to hold our heads up."

Brad felt something snap deep inside him and realized it was his self-control. He would not bite his tongue. This time Father had gone too far. "If I fail, it's my failure, not yours," he said. His voice sounded like a stranger's, hard and determined. "If that bothers you, you can pretend you don't know me." Father blinked in surprise, then opened his mouth to speak. Forestalling him, Brad shook his head. "If you think you can intimidate me and make me abandon my plans, you're wrong. I will do this, and I will succeed." Brad turned his gaze from his father to his mother. Her eyes filled with tears as she realized this was one rift she could not heal. "I had hoped for your approval. Obviously I was wrong in thinking I'd ever get that."

As his father started to sputter, Brad looked at him, hoping against hope he'd see understanding. Instead, disappointment and anger radiated from the head of the table. Father would never change. It was time Brad accepted that. "You want things done your way and won't even consider that another idea might be worthwhile." Years of frustration colored Brad's words. "I've tried to please you, but I'm done. It's taken me a long time to realize that pleasing you is impossible. I can never succeed, so I won't even try again." Brad pushed back his chair.

His father rose, fury etched on his face. "Don't take that tone with me, young man. I'm your father."

"I can't forget that, but you needn't worry. You won't have daily reminders of me and all the disappointment I've caused."

"What do you mean?" Mother's face had turned white, and he saw raw pain in her eyes.

"I'm going to move out."

For once Father was silent. It was Mother who cried, "But where will you go?"

"Anywhere would be better than this."

Tears streaming down her face, Brad's mother clutched her husband's arm. "Jacob, can't you stop him?"

It was Brad who replied. "No, Mother, he cannot. No one can stop me. I'm going to start my newspaper, and I will succeed."

"So where is the girl?" Abel's experience told him that Clifford Warren was not a patient man, and today was no exception. In defiance of convention, he'd arrived at the house before the breakfast hour, announcing he would not leave until he had some answers. Now, seated at the long table, a plate heaped with food in front of him, he glared at Abel. "Don't tell me she's ailing. I won't buy that tale any longer."

It was time for the truth, unpleasant though it might be. "She's gone," Abel admitted. "Don't worry, though," he added quickly, lest the man who was vital to his plans decide there were other heiresses he might marry. "She'll soon be back. She has no money, and she didn't take her clothing or jewelry." That had surprised Abel almost as much as the girl's disappearance. Of course he had no intention of telling Clifford that. The man was supposed to consider Eleanor the perfect wife. "Don't worry," he repeated. "The pampered chit can't live long without them."

Clifford shoveled a forkful of scrambled egg into his mouth, chewing loudly. "I don't like this. You said Missy was biddable. This shenanigan makes me think she's headstrong and spoiled." Clifford reached for another piece of toast. "I tell you, Abel, I don't want to be saddled with a wife like that, no matter how much money she brings me."

Though the man's assessment of Abel's niece was accurate, he would not admit that. Clifford was part of the plan. One way or another, Abel had to convince him the reward would be worth this temporary inconvenience. "Think of it this way: You won't be saddled with her for long if you don't want to be." Abel gave his friend a wolfish grin. "Accidents can happen."

Chapter Three

Though it was still May, the evening held the heat and humidity of July, or so Deborah claimed. She and Eleanor had climbed the stairs to their room, only to discover living proof that heat rises. The attic was stifling, and opening the window only brought more warm air into an already sweltering room.

"This is one of the few times I wish I was still on the farm," Deborah said as she settled onto her bed and fanned herself in a vain attempt to cool her flushed face. "It seemed like there was always a breeze there. I used to sit under this big old oak tree." She smiled, apparently enjoying her memories. "I would take off my shoes and bury my toes in the grass. Ma used to complain it wasn't ladylike, but one time she sat right down beside me and did the same thing." Deborah chuckled. "We didn't tell Pa, though."

It was a tale as foreign to Eleanor as Charles Dickens's stories of English orphans. When the weather grew hot in New York, she and her mother would move to the seashore. But never once did she recall Mama removing her shoes. It was unthinkable that a lady would uncover her hands in public. As for her feet? Eleanor could picture Mama's delicate shudder at the very thought.

"Let's go outside. I'm sure we can find some shade." Anything had to be cooler than this room.

"The park will be crowded," Deborah said as they descended the stairs. "Everyone wants to ride the carousel."

Though Eleanor had been intrigued by the stories of the town's new merry-go-round, her legs ached almost unbearably from the long days at the mill. The swelling had subsided, but her limbs were still unaccustomed to ten hours of labor. Simply standing that long took its toll on her calves. "I don't think I can walk that far," she told Deborah. "Let's find someplace else." Outside the temperature was a few degrees cooler with the faintest of breezes. Eleanor surveyed the area, smiling when she spotted a likely destination. "There it is: our private park." She gestured toward a small patch of grass on the east side of the boardinghouse.

The look Deborah gave her reminded Eleanor of Mama on those occasions when Eleanor had said something her mother considered outrageous. "No one sits there."

"Why not?" Though lacking benches and other park amenities, the spot Eleanor had chosen had the advantages of shade, proximity to the boardinghouse, and solitude. The only disadvantage was the location of the men's boardinghouse across the street, but at this time of the evening, the men were all gone. For a few minutes at least, she and Deborah would have privacy.

"C'mon, Deborah." Eleanor sank onto the grass, then tugged on her friend's hand. "We'll look like that Manet painting, *Le déjeuner sur l'herbe*." She wouldn't mention that the woman in the painting was unclothed or how Mama had blushed when Eleanor had crossed the room to stare at it.

"You speak French." Deborah lowered herself to the grass and stared at Eleanor as if she had suddenly sprouted horns.

Dumb, Eleanor. Dumb. You're supposed to be a shop-keeper's daughter. "My mother used to take me to art museums, and she insisted that I learn the names of the paintings." Once again, she'd uttered a half-truth, but— if she was fortunate—Deborah wouldn't ask for details. She didn't need to know about the years Eleanor had spent in a private school or how she'd learned both French and German. What they needed was a diversion. "I think we're overdressed," Eleanor said.

Lines formed between Deborah's eyes. "What do you mean?"

"Shoes." Eleanor pointed toward her feet. "You're the one who gave me the idea, you know." She began to unlace her boots. Suddenly nothing seemed more important than wriggling her toes in the grass. Deborah stared at her for a second before she tugged off her own footwear.

"Ummm." Eleanor sighed with pleasure. The grass was as thick as one of her mother's treasured Aubusson carpets, but carpets never smelled so fresh and sweet. Carpets weren't this lush green. And, most important, carpets didn't tickle her instep or send shivers up her legs. Who would have believed such a simple act could bring so much pleasure? Eleanor had had summers by the sea and autumn trips to the mountains. She'd toured museums and attended concerts and ballets, but she'd never before walked barefoot in the grass.

"I've never been to an art museum." Eleanor blinked, wondering whether Deborah had somehow read her thoughts. Nonsense. It was simply that she still remembered Eleanor's unfortunate comment.

"There are a lot of museums in New York." As two men walked by, tipping their hats to the women, Eleanor tucked her feet beneath her skirt. From this distance, it was unlikely anyone would notice the boots sitting by her side.

Deborah followed suit. "Did you know that Mr. Moreland's wife is an artist? She even studied in Paris."

Intrigued, Eleanor wished she could meet the mill owner's wife and ask her whether she'd visited the Louvre. But that would never happen. Owners didn't mingle with mill hands. It was true Brad Harrod had spoken to the passengers on the train, but that was business. Undoubtedly Mr. Moreland would greet mill workers if he encountered them at the factory. Socializing in other situations was a far different matter. "Do you ever see Mrs. Moreland?" she asked Deborah.

"Oh, yes. She and Mr. Moreland come to church every Sunday, and last Thanksgiving they had a party for all of us." Deborah dug her toes more deeply into the grass. "You wouldn't believe how nice she and Miss Jane Moreland were to Virginia and me. They treated us just like we were one of them, even if we don't live in a fancy house on the hill."

"They wouldn't have a fancy house if it weren't for you." Did the Morelands and the Harrods realize that? Eleanor wasn't certain they did. Her father had never talked about the people whose labor created his wealth, and he'd certainly never hosted a party for them.

Deborah gave her a long look. "You sound like Matt Wagner. He was always trying to get Mr. Moreland to improve conditions at the mill."

Matt Wagner was an unfamiliar name, and Eleanor found herself intrigued. "Why did he stop?"

"When he married Jane Moreland, they moved to New York City." Deborah lowered her voice to a conspiratorial level. "It was all anybody could talk about. We all figured she'd marry Brad Harrod. His father owns the railroad, you know. Then Jane up and married Matt. Nothing against Matt, but his father was a mill worker just like Virginia and me. We never figured someone from the hill would marry one of us."

Matt, Eleanor learned as she wiggled her toes in the grass, had earned a law degree from Harvard. Despite that, in the eyes of the town, he would always be a mill hand's son. Even worse, he was a mill hand's son with a reputation for a rather wild youth. The combination had had a decidedly deleterious effect on his law practice. It was no wonder Matt had chosen to leave Hidden Falls for the anonymity of a large city.

"I heard the Harrods were mighty disappointed when Jane didn't marry their son." Deborah continued the story. "Now that Anne Moreland is married, there's no one left in Hidden Falls for Brad."

As Deborah spoke, Eleanor pictured Uncle Abel the day she'd told him she would not marry Clifford Warren. It wasn't disappointment she'd seen on his face, but pure fury. "Mama always told me I should marry for love," she said softly.

"My ma said the same thing." Deborah leaned forward, her smile dreamy. "When I used to ask her how I'd know if it was true love, she said she couldn't explain it, but I'd know when it happened."

"And now you're planning to marry Franklin, so you must have figured it out."

"Oh, yes!" Deborah's smile widened. "My heart races every time I see him, and when he smiles at me, I feel as if my legs have turned to rubber."

That sounded uncomfortable, not to mention inconvenient, but who was Eleanor to judge? She'd never been in love. "Have you set a wedding date?"

"Not yet. We've talked about Christmas, but it all depends on whether we can save enough money by then."

As the unmistakable sound of an internal combustion engine drew closer, Eleanor turned to Deborah. "Does someone in Hidden Falls have a motorcar?" Though common in New York City, she had seen none of Henry Ford's creations here.

Deborah craned her neck. "It's Brad Harrod," she announced when she was able to identify the driver. "I wonder what he's doing here."

The car slowed as it passed them. Though he was looking the opposite way, there was no mistaking him. The driver was none other than the man who had spoken to Eleanor on the train, the man she now knew was Brad Harrod, scion of the Harrod railroad family. He slowed the car further, then parked it next to the men's boardinghouse.

"It must be true," Deborah said softly. "I heard he'd moved out of his parents' house, but I didn't know he was living here."

Eleanor tried to hide her surprise that one of Hidden Falls' aristocracy was living in a mill workers' boardinghouse. That did not fit the picture she had formed of Brad Harrod. Of course, it didn't matter any more than it mattered that she thought of him at the oddest times, replaying his brief conversation with her, seeing his expression when she turned back to her paper rather than speak with him. How she wished she hadn't snubbed him.

The man in question headed for the boardinghouse, then, apparently catching sight of Eleanor and Deborah, made an abrupt turn and crossed the street.

"Good evening, ladies." Though his voice remained neutral, Eleanor saw the moment he recognized her. Surprise and something else—could it be amusement?—flitted across his face. It must have been her imagination, for there was no reason for amusement. "May I join you?"

As Deborah gave Eleanor a look that said more clearly than words she wished she were a hundred miles away, Eleanor realized the situation did have its amusing aspect. Nothing in her years of social training had prepared her for this. Though it would be rude to ignore Mr. Harrod, they couldn't stand to greet him, for if they did, their bare feet would be obvious. That would be an even greater breach of decorum than ignoring a gentleman. At Eleanor's side, Deborah moved nervously. "Why do you want to join us?" Deborah's voice reflected suspicion as well as discomfort.

Brad Harrod's eyes flickered with surprise at the question, then moved slowly, perhaps searching for the right spot of lawn to claim as his own. When his lips started to curve upward, Eleanor realized he'd seen their boots and understood their significance. If he mentioned them, Deborah would be mortified. Eleanor couldn't let that happen.

"Mr. Harrod is a gregarious soul," she said smoothly. "He saw us sitting alone and probably thought we needed some entertainment."

"You've wounded me, Miss. . . ." He let his voice trail off, obviously angling for an introduction. Thank goodness he was no longer looking at their boots!

Her nervousness apparently dissipating, Deborah

spoke. "She's Eleanor Menger, and I'm Deborah Sempert."

"As I was saying, Miss Menger." Brad Harrod accompanied his words with a wry smile, silently reminding Eleanor of the first time they'd met. "Your assumption wounded me. The fact is, no man could resist the opportunity to spend a few minutes with two such beautiful young ladies." He placed his hand on his heart as he sighed deeply. "My life will be incomplete if you refuse me, and I shall expire from disappointment. Imagine the distress it would cause Hidden Falls' citizens to find one of their number had given up the ghost right here where everyone could see." His words were outrageous, and yet Eleanor couldn't help enjoying them. The men she knew were all serious. Not one of them would have resorted to melodrama simply to attract her attention. "Think of it this way," he continued. "You'll be performing a public service."

"And it would be positively churlish to refuse," Eleanor said, barely resisting the urge to laugh.

As Brad Harrod grinned, his eyes took on a deep emerald hue. "I venture to say that you, Miss Menger, are never churlish."

"Never, Mr. Harrod,"—*except for that unfortunate meeting on the train,* Eleanor added silently—"and neither is Deborah. We would be honored to have you join us for a brief conversation on the grass."

As he settled a discreet distance from them, stretching his long legs in front of him, Deborah laughed. "You two are so funny. I didn't know people talked like that."

They didn't. At least not in normal conversation, but the flowery phrases were a part of the courting ritual that Eleanor had been taught to expect. One of the very expensive schools Mama had chosen conducted a course in the art of courtship conversation. Not that this was a courtship. Of course it was not. It was simply that Brad Harrod was a product of the same educational system.

"It comes from living in the city," Eleanor said, hoping Deborah would accept the explanation. As she'd gotten to know her fellow workers, she'd discovered that most people with rural backgrounds believed city dwellers were a different species.

"Or from reading newspapers." He smiled again, his eyes darkening once more. "I must thank you, Miss Menger. Your fascination with a newspaper made me decide to start my own."

Eleanor blinked, certain he was joking. Surely her cowardly refuge behind a paper had inspired nothing more than contempt on his part.

"We're going to have a paper here?" Deborah's voice held both surprise and delight.

"Yes, indeed." He was serious. By some miracle, her rudeness had served a positive purpose. "I expect it will be the finest in the state."

Relief rushed through Eleanor's veins as she realized that he hadn't been insulted. "Why be so modest?" she asked. "Surely your paper will be the finest in the whole United States of America."

"Why, Miss Menger, I do believe you are mocking me."

"You must be mistaken, sir. Surely I would never do such a despicable thing."

Their laughter formed a chorus, lightening Eleanor's heart. How long had it been since she'd laughed like this? She couldn't recall. All she knew was that it felt wonderful to be sitting here, joking and laughing with this man. Not once had any of her suitors made her laugh. Not once had any of them challenged her or made her feel alive. Not once had she had a real conversation with any of them. This was different. Of course it was, for Brad Harrod was not a suitor. Not now. Not ever.

He couldn't get her out of his mind, and that was absurd, totally absurd. After all, there were many other things to occupy his mind, far more important things. There was the printing press scheduled to arrive on the first train tomorrow. There were the employees he planned to hire before the week ended. And there was all that he'd learned on his trip to New York.

From the beginning, Brad had been determined to master every aspect of the newspaper process, from writing copy to typesetting to printing and delivery of the finished product, and so he'd gone to New York to spend some time at one of the major papers. They'd been accommodating, letting him actually participate rather than merely observe. And in the doing, he'd discovered producing a newspaper was a dirty, noisy process. He'd also found it to be the most exhilarating experience of his life. He would never have thought that writing a one-inch advertisement and following it from concept to newsprint would be so fulfilling. Though it had taken him minutes to do what an experienced typesetter could have done in seconds, once he'd written the copy, Brad had taken it to the Linotype machine and had set the type.

How fascinating it was to watch as the type was cast into a mold and to observe the speed with which paper fed through the presses. When he'd held the finished newspaper in his hands and read his advertisement, Brad had practically crowed with pleasure. This was what he wanted to do.

And then, unbidden, he'd thought of Miss Eleanor Menger and wondered what she would say if she could see him, standing there grinning at a piece of newsprint. Would she be amused by his fascination with the whole process, or would she understand how important it had become to him? It shouldn't matter, of course. What mattered was that this was what Brad wanted to do. This was the life he'd chosen.

He looked around the small room that was now his home. When he'd arrived at the boardinghouse, he'd expected to share a room with the mill hands. But that idea, he soon discovered, had horrified his house-mother. Mrs. Larimer had shaken her head, announcing that Mr. Harrod—she refused to call him by his given name—could not possibly do that. Instead, she had cleared out the first-floor pantry and arranged for a bed and washstand to be placed there. And all the while, she'd been muttering under her breath that it was only for a short time. Like everyone else in Hidden Falls,

Mrs. Larimer was certain Brad would soon return home. Even Charles, who'd offered him a room in his house when he learned Brad had moved out of his parents' home, had made it clear he thought the arrangement would be temporary. But it was not. Though his living quarters were cramped and the food, while plentiful, lacked the variety and flavor of the meals his mother's French chef served, there was no denying the fact that Brad felt more alive here than ever before.

It had nothing to do with the fact that the intriguing Miss Eleanor Menger lived across the street. Of course it didn't. There was no reason why his thoughts should continue to return to her, why he should recall her smile or the way she'd studiously avoided looking at her boots, obviously hoping he wouldn't notice that she and her companion were barefoot. His mother, always a stickler for propriety, would have been appalled. But Mother was easily appalled. The one time she'd come to the boardinghouse, begging Brad to return home, her face had paled at the sight of the crowded conditions. Her son, she had announced, had no need to live in such squalor. She refused to understand that it wasn't squalor. It was simply a different kind of existence, one Brad found refreshing.

He reached for his hat and strode outside, looking carefully at the boardinghouse across the street. It was nothing more than idle curiosity, of course. It wasn't as if he were looking for anyone in particular. It wasn't as if he had hoped that Miss Eleanor Menger would be sitting on the grass, her shoes carefully placed at her side. She wasn't. It was Sunday afternoon, the one time no one was working. More than that, it was a perfectly beautiful Sunday afternoon, not too hot, not too windy, just right for a stroll in the park and a ride on the town's new carousel. Undoubtedly that was what Miss Menger was doing.

Brad turned right and headed for the center of town, pausing when he reached the corner of Rapids Street. Which way would she have gone? Would she continue on Main or take Rapids to Mill? It was ridiculous to care, just as it was ridiculous the way his thoughts turned to this one woman so often.

Eleanor was beautiful, but so were a hundred other women. Her beauty wasn't what fascinated him. When he'd first met her, Brad had named her The Mystery Woman. Though the conversation they'd shared on the grass should have dissipated that mystery, it had only enhanced it, for it had illuminated the fact that Eleanor was unlike other mill workers. Her diction, her bearing, even her hands were different from those of her companion. Oh, it was true she had cuts on her hands, the result of the hours she spent in the mill, but her fingers lacked the calluses and the coarser skin that seemed characteristic of women who worked for a living. No doubt about it, Eleanor was an anomaly.

It wasn't only her appearance that intrigued him. He might have forgotten how her green eyes sparkled or how the skin on the bridge of her nose crinkled when she smiled. He might have forgotten the four freckles that dotted one cheek, but he could not forget the way she'd sparred with him. She was quick and witty, and Brad could not recall a conversation he'd enjoyed as much as the one they'd shared.

Before he reached Bridge Street, he heard the sound of the Würlitzer organ. Charles had told him the music was like a siren's song, luring people to the carousel. Surely this was where Eleanor had come. Not that he was looking for her. Brad shook his head. There was no point in deluding himself. He'd come here for the express purpose of finding Miss Eleanor Menger. He knew that if he spent a few more minutes in her company, he'd discover there was nothing special about her, and then she would no longer haunt his thoughts.

There she was! Though several dozen people clustered around the merry-go-round, Brad's eyes were drawn to only one. It was annoying the way his pulse leaped at the sight of her. After all, he was a grown man, no longer a youth, the ebb and flow of his emotions triggered by a pretty face. He should be able to maintain his composure, and yet, though his brain urged caution, his feet paid no heed. They rushed him toward Miss Eleanor Menger. She stood between two other women. Brad recognized one as her companion of the other night. The other's facial features announced she was the companion's sister.

"May I join you?" Brad doffed his hat when he reached the trio. Though he included all three in his greeting, his eyes lingered on Eleanor. She was taller than the others, standing an inch or so higher than he'd expected. This was, Brad realized, the first time he'd seen her on her feet—properly shod feet, a quick glance revealed.

She saw the direction of his gaze and smiled, a smile that made his heart race faster than the motor of his Model T. "Is this another public service?" she asked.

Public service? It took only a fraction of a second for Brad to realize she was referring to that absurd bantering they'd shared. His heart soared again at the thought that he wasn't the only one who'd remembered the details of their meeting. He shook his head in response to her question. "Not today. Today it would be my personal pleasure to have the honor of your company for a few minutes." Though he placed only the slightest emphasis on "personal," her lips twitched in apparent amusement.

Eleanor turned to her companions. Though Brad saw no nodding, they must have agreed with her, for she said, "We would be pleased to have you join us. I must warn you, though, that we intend to ride the carousel."

"Who could resist Rob Ludlow's finest creation?" Brad had spent hours in the carousel carver's workshop while he was building the merry-go-round Charles had commissioned for his sister, and those hours had given him a deep appreciation for the talent required to design, carve, and paint a carousel horse.

"Which animal do you fancy?" When they reached the front of the line and entered the pavilion, the sisters headed for a pair of horses, leaving Eleanor with Brad. She tipped her head to the right, gesturing toward her choice.

"Let's ride the ostriches." Unlike some carousels, which consisted exclusively of horses, Rob Ludlow had created what carvers called a menagerie. In addition to eight pairs of horses, his merry-go-round featured a pair each of ostriches, bears, elephants, and giraffes.

"An excellent choice." Though Charles claimed that the giraffes were his and Susannah's favorites, Brad had always been drawn to the ostriches. He couldn't explain it. With their long yellow legs and necks, they looked a bit ungainly and reminded him of the years when his legs had seemed too long for his body. Perhaps that was what appealed to him. But surely Eleanor had never been a gangly youth.

Brad helped her onto the inside ostrich before taking his seat on the larger outside one. Though the outside one was more elaborately decorated and should, in Brad's opinion, be given to a lady, both Charles and Rob had informed him that gentlemen rode the outside animals. It was, they explained, a carryover from the Middle Ages when knights used carousels to hone their fighting skills. Being positioned on the outside meant a knight's sword arm was ready to defend his lady. Though twentieth-century Hidden Falls was blessedly free from crime, Brad could not deny the appeal of being a knight in shining armor, saving Eleanor's honor.

"Are you ready, my lady?"

If his salutation surprised her, she gave no sign, merely smiled again and grasped the brass pole. As the carousel began to revolve, Brad grinned. Charles had once claimed no one could be unhappy on a merry-go-round and that that was the reason he wanted his sister Anne, who'd suffered so much, to have one. Brad could not dispute his hypothesis. There was something soothing, something almost magical, about the gentle up-and-down motion of the animals. Or perhaps the magic came from his companion, for her enjoyment of the ride seemed contagious.

"That was wonderful," Eleanor said as he helped her dismount.

"Your first carousel ride?"

She shook her head, the motion causing a tendril of hair to bounce against her neck. Though it would be unseemly in the extreme, Brad's fingers longed to touch the errant strand, to discover whether it was as soft as it appeared. Mercifully oblivious to his thoughts, Eleanor said, "I rode one on Coney Island, but this is the first time I've been on an ostrich."

He took her hand as they stepped off the carousel platform, carefully releasing it as soon as she was on level ground. There was no point in setting tongues a-wagging, no matter how much he would have liked to keep Eleanor's hand clasped in his. "We'll have to ensure that it's not your last." Another ride on an ostrich was as good an excuse as any for spending more time with her. Today was supposed to be like an inoculation, making him immune to her. So far, it wasn't working, but perhaps the vaccine needed more time to take effect. "Would you like to stroll around the park before we ride again?"

Though she nodded as they left the pavilion, Eleanor

waited until the sisters rejoined them. That wasn't part of Brad's plan. If he was going to cure himself of thoughts of Eleanor, he needed time alone with her. He addressed the sisters. "I have asked Miss Menger to join me on a short walk and then another ride on the merry-go-round." Though he didn't voice the word *alone,* he saw that they understood. "I assure you that I'll see her safely back to your boardinghouse."

The sisters exchanged a glance before the older said, "Deborah and I were a bit fatigued and discussed returning home, but we didn't want to shorten Eleanor's first time on the carousel. We had promised her at least two rides."

Though Brad suspected the story was false, he was grateful the sisters didn't insist on chaperoning Eleanor. "Your friends are very kind," he said when they'd left the park.

"They are indeed, Mr. Harrod."

As Brad crooked his arm, she placed her hand on it. Why had he never noticed how warm a woman's hand could be and how the lightest of touches sent sparks shooting through him?

"Would you call me Brad?" Mr. Harrod was his father.

She raised an eyebrow. "That would be most unconventional."

Shrugging, he said, "I believe we've already established that I'm unconventional." How else would you describe the fact that he'd approached her on the train and again when she'd been seated in the grass?

"All right . . ." She hesitated before adding, "Brad."

"May I be doubly unconventional and call you Eleanor?" When she nodded, Brad's pulse accelerated again. Could she feel that through her gloves and his jacket and shirt? He certainly hoped not. He'd best speak of ordinary things if he wanted to keep his heart rate under control. "I'd like to talk to you about my newspaper."

"Because I'm fascinated by them?" she asked, emphasizing the adjective.

Brad's heart lurched at yet another indication that she'd remembered their last conversation. "In part, yes."

"And what would the other part be?"

"I'd like your insights into a large group of my potential readers: the mill hands. I want to feature them in occasional articles, and I thought you might be able to help me." Where had that thought come from? It was an intriguing idea, but five minutes ago Brad had not considered the possibility. Once again this woman was providing inspiration.

She shook her head, making him fear she disapproved of the articles. But when she spoke, her words reassured him. "I have so little experience that I don't think I could represent them well."

She was wrong. "That very lack of experience means you're not blasé. You see things with a different perspective than someone who's been working there for two years."

They were at the west end of the park now, in full sight of other visitors but far enough away that their conversation would not be overheard. She stopped and looked up at him, a question in her green eyes. "That's probably true. But I still don't understand how I can help you."

Brad took a deep breath, hoping he'd be able to explain his vision properly, hoping that she'd approve of it. "Everyone knows I'm starting a paper," he told her. "What few know is that I want to make reading it an enjoyable experience."

Both eyebrows rose in surprise. "Isn't 'enjoyable news' an oxymoron?"

"Maybe elsewhere, but that won't be true of the *Hidden Falls Herald*. I want to present positive news to show people that life here is good. I want them to laugh."

As he'd hoped, Eleanor nodded. "It's an admirable goal. We all need more laughter in our lives."

"But if I'm going to succeed, I have to understand what mill workers would find humorous."

"You seem to think they're . . ." Quickly she corrected herself, an odd, almost furtive, expression crossing her face. It was gone so quickly Brad thought he must have imagined it. "You seem to think *we're* different from other people," she said with a hint of asperity. "That's not true."

Brad chastised himself mentally. He'd obviously insulted Eleanor, when that was the last thing he'd intended. "That was not what I meant. I agree with you that people are people, regardless of the way they earn their living. It's simply that I know amusing things must happen at the mill, but I'm not privy to them."

He could feel her hand relax. "You mean like the morning I was wearing a freshly laundered apron? It was white, of course. By some perverse stroke of fate, that was the day I decided to help water the plants. The next thing I knew, a huge pot had tumbled down, and my white apron was covered with wet black soil." Eleanor gave him a self-deprecating smile. "Apparently that happens to everyone once, so they all laughed and told me I'd been initiated."

Brad nodded, encouraging her. "That's exactly what I meant when I said I needed your perspective. More experienced workers have probably forgotten their first time with the plants." He was silent for a moment, thinking of what she'd said. "I want to use your anecdote, but I don't want to stop there. This could become a regular feature in the paper, how people were initiated into their jobs. Everyone in town could contribute stories." When Eleanor appeared a bit skeptical, he explained, "They wouldn't have to worry about writing them. I'd do that, but they'd give me their ideas."

She nodded, her enthusiasm evident. "It would be a wonderful way to bring the town together."

"And sell some papers too." Brad made his words as dry as he could, hoping she'd laugh. She did.

"Be careful." As Virginia pulled the pins from her hair, she gave Eleanor an appraising look. The two women were in their room, preparing for bed, while Deborah remained downstairs, writing a letter to Franklin.

"Careful?" Eleanor had already completed her ablutions and was resting. "What do you mean?"

"Be careful of Brad Harrod. I don't want him to hurt you." Though neither Virginia nor Deborah had asked about her time with Brad while they were in the dining room and could be overheard, Eleanor had seen the curiosity in both of their eyes, and she'd expected Virginia to make some comment. She had not expected concern.

"I could only be hurt if I had unrealistic expectations," Eleanor said slowly. "I assure you, Virginia, I have none of those. Brad's a charming companion, and I'd be lying if I said I didn't enjoy being with him. I do. He makes me laugh, and that's good, but I know I'm nothing more than a temporary diversion for him." Four different women had told her about his failed romance with Jane Moreland and the rift with his parents that had driven him to move out of the family home. "As for me," Eleanor continued, "I'm only going to be here for a year. Then I'll return to New York." And a life that would not include Brad any more than it would include Uncle Abel and Clifford Warren. "I'm not foolish enough to think there's any future for me with Brad Harrod."

In another world, there might have been, but this was not another world.

Chapter Four

"Slow down, Eleanor. I need to talk to you."

She turned, surprised to see Millie Trimble pushing her way through the crowd of women. It was the end of the workday, and they were all anxious for supper and a chance to relax before the next day began. Each evening was the same. First the mill's stairwells rang with the clatter of hundreds of pairs of shoes. Then the crowd fanned out as they exited the building, only to contract again at the gate. It was, Eleanor had often thought, like a tidal surge, powerful enough to knock down anything in its path. At less than five feet tall and slender to the point of gauntness, Millie was small enough to be lost in the supper rush.

"I'm sorry," Eleanor said when the petite blond who shared her table at the boardinghouse reached her. "I didn't realize I was going so fast."

"You do everything fast." Millie's words came out in bursts as she tried to catch her breath. "Don't you fret none. That's a compliment. I heard Virginia tell Mr. Greeley you learned faster than any apprentice she's trained."

"Really?" Eleanor couldn't help being pleased. "I thought she was just saying that to encourage me." In Eleanor's estimation, Virginia was a born teacher. No matter how many mistakes Eleanor made, Virginia never became impatient. Instead, she declared that each mistake was a learning experience and that the goal was not to repeat that particular error.

"It's true." Millie emphasized her words with a firm nod. "You're already running a loom by yourself. Pretty soon you'll have two like the rest of us. Difference is, it took us a whole lot longer than one month to master a loom. You're a wonder, Eleanor."

The rush of pleasure sweeping through Eleanor startled her with its intensity. Though her parents would be shocked if they could see her now, her hands marred with scars and tiny blisters, her feet shod in sensible boots rather than delicate kidskin pumps, she couldn't deny the satisfaction she felt over having done a job well. For the first time in her life, she was engaged in something useful. Instead of painting watercolors that no one would ever see or playing sonatas that lulled the gentlemen to sleep, she was making fabric destined to become sheets and towels in some of the country's finest homes and hotels.

"Thank you for saying that."

"Now you'll think I'm buttering you up. That weren't my intention. Honest." As they crossed the street surrounded by the other workers, Millie looked up at Eleanor, her eyes shining with integrity. "I just figured you could help us."

"Help you with what?"

"The Independence Day celebration. There's always a big parade. Some of the girls was talking about how we wanted to be in the parade too. You know, kind of like we was part of the town."

Eleanor heard the longing in Millie's voice, and she understood the cause. Though almost everyone in Hidden Falls was polite to the mill hands, there was no denying they were treated differently from the other citizens. Eleanor had noticed that the first time she'd entered the general store. Two women, their hats proclaiming their owners' membership in the elite group of Hidden Falls' well-to-do, were waited on before the mill workers, despite the fact that Eleanor and her friends had been there longer. The fancy-hatted women were the recipients of inquiries about their families, while Eleanor received nothing more than a "thank you" when she paid her bill. She suspected the situation was no different in New York. The difference was, she had been a favored customer there, and, though it shamed her to admit it, she had never noticed that others were not treated with the same courtesy.

When she'd mentioned the disparity to Deborah and Virginia, they'd shrugged and told her that was simply the way it was. Judging from Millie's comment, though the mill workers might have accepted their lower status in town, they didn't like it. Eleanor agreed. If participating in the Independence Day parade changed the rest of Hidden Falls' perception of the mill workers, even if only slightly, it was worth any effort involved.

"That's a great idea," she told Millie. "How can I help?"

"We don't know how to get started. I reckoned you might have some ideas, being from a big city and all. We're meetin' tonight in the other boardinghouse."

"I'll be there."

When the meeting began, there were only three other women there: Millie and two who lived in the second boardinghouse. Eleanor had thought there would be more, just as she'd assumed Millie would lead the discussion. Instead, to Eleanor's surprise, they all deferred to her. Though at first she found the role awkward, Eleanor soon discovered it was a heady feeling, being valued for herself rather than her surname or her trust fund.

"Tell me about the Hidden Falls parades," she urged the others. Though she'd seen countless parades in New York City, the ones here would undoubtedly differ in some respects.

"All the schoolchildren are there," the blond told Eleanor. "They sing 'The Star-Spangled Banner' while they're marching."

"Not very well," Millie pointed out, "but no one seems to mind."

The dark-haired woman's face lit with pleasure as

she said, "There are always a few floats. One of them is covered with flags."

"Of course the band plays music," the blond added. "You can hear that all over town."

When they'd exhausted their descriptions, Eleanor asked, "What would you like to do?"

"Ride a float," the brunet said without hesitation.

"I agree." Both Millie and the blond nodded their heads.

It was what Eleanor had feared. She'd seen the enthusiasm on the three women's faces when they spoke of the floats' beauty. No one seemed to have considered the practical aspects.

"We'll need a wagon and horses," she pointed out. "Do you know where we could get those?"

The blond's face fell. "I hadn't thought of that."

The women's disappointment wrenched Eleanor's heart. They worked so hard and received so little in return. If she knew how to construct a float, she would do it, but she didn't. Instead, she tried to give the women an alternative. "Floats are beautiful," Eleanor said, "but only a few people can ride on one." Though she didn't voice the thought, a float would divide the workers into two groups: those who rode and those who did not. Wasn't their goal to erase distinctions rather than create them? "If we marched, everyone could participate. We'd all be part of the celebration."

Eleanor saw by the way the three women smiled that they were convinced. "That would be good." As the brunet pronounced the words, the others nodded.

"If we want people to really notice us, we all need to dress the same." Eleanor had already established that the schoolchildren did not do that.

"Something red, white, and blue," Millie suggested.

"I agree." This was, after all, the most patriotic of holidays. "I imagine everyone has a navy skirt and a white shirtwaist. What do we have that's red?"

"Hats?" As she made the suggestion, the blond raised her hand to her head, as if settling a hat on it.

The dark-haired woman shook her head. "I don't own a red hat, and it would be a waste of money to buy one. I'd never wear it again."

As she recalled one of the parades she'd seen, Eleanor nodded slowly. "I have an idea," she told the others, "but I don't want to raise your hopes until I'm sure it will work. Will you give me two days to find us the perfect red for our costumes?"

The others agreed, and a few minutes later, the meeting broke up. "I was right." Millie squeezed Eleanor's hand. "I knew you'd have good ideas."

The compliment made Eleanor smile with pleasure. As she left the boardinghouse, she glanced across the street, remembering a different kind of pleasure. It had become a habit, looking in the direction of the former warehouse that Brad had turned into his newspaper plant each time she left the mill. Since the day they had ridden the carousel together, Eleanor had seen Brad almost daily. Their conversations were necessarily brief, for he was working feverishly to get all of his equipment installed and could spare little time for anything not directly related to his newspaper, but somehow the enforced brevity made their encounters all the more memorable. Eleanor felt as if they were distilling their days' experiences into a few words. And, as with all distillations, that made each one more potent.

She frowned slightly when she saw a light still burning in the newspaper office. Brad had said nothing about working so late tonight. The first issue of the paper was scheduled to be printed tomorrow morning. Though Brad had claimed everything would be done by normal closing time, it appeared something was wrong. Eleanor's heart began to race as she considered what might have gone amiss. The production process was so complex, it could be almost anything. She frowned again at the realization that no matter how much she wondered what Brad was doing, she couldn't visit him unchaperoned. That would be unseemly, and so she turned toward her boardinghouse. But only seconds later, Eleanor found herself glancing back. This time the light was gone, and a man strode toward her. She stopped, smiling, and waited for him to join her.

"Eleanor!" Brad's voice was as warm as a summer afternoon. "What are you doing out so late?"

"I could ask you the same question."

He slowed his pace to match hers as they turned onto Rapid Street. "I was checking—and double-checking—every line. It may sound silly, but I think I'm as nervous as my friend Charles. And that is silly, because he has a reason and I don't. After all, Charles is an expectant father."

"So are you . . . in a way." Eleanor couldn't picture Brad cradling a pile of newspapers in his arms, but she knew he regarded the whole enterprise as part of himself. It wasn't too farfetched to say the *Herald* was his offspring. "Are you afraid your baby will be ugly?"

"Something like that."

She tightened her grip on Brad's arm ever so slightly, hoping the warmth of her hand would reassure him. "It's time to stop worrying. First of all, you can't change anything now. And, more important, everything you've showed me was wonderful. I expect the *Herald* to be a resounding success."

"I hope you're right. One way or another, we'll know tomorrow." Brad's use of the plural pronoun set Eleanor's pulse racing. He was acting as though she was part of the process. While it was true she'd offered some suggestions, her role had been primarily supportive.

Brad cocked his head toward the boardinghouse. "What were you doing here tonight? I thought you had planned to go the library with Virginia."

"I had, but Millie Trimble invited me to a meeting." Quickly, Eleanor explained how the mill workers wanted to be part of the parade. "What do we have to do?" she asked. Even though Hidden Falls was a small town, she suspected there were some formalities involved.

"You just tell Mayor McBride you want to march. I suppose that officially you're asking permission, but it's mostly a courtesy visit. I'm sure he'll agree." Brad pursed his lips for a second, as if he were considering something. "I have another idea," he said. By unspoken consent they'd slowed their steps, prolonging the short walk back to Eleanor's boardinghouse. Now Brad stopped, the gleam in his eyes revealing his enthusiasm. "What if your part in the parade were a surprise? I could print hints about the mysterious participants in the paper and keep everyone guessing your identity." As if he sensed Eleanor's question, Brad added, "You wouldn't have to worry about the mayor; I'll talk to him."

It took only a second for Eleanor to nod. "What a brilliant idea! The girls will be excited and you . . ." She paused for dramatic emphasis. "You'll sell more papers."

"Exactly."

They were still laughing when they said good night.

Eleanor wasn't certain what caused more excitement in the weaving room the next day, the idea of being part of the parade or the first edition of the *Hidden Falls Herald.* The women had all bought copies of the paper on their dinner break, reading them surreptitiously as they ate and then openly as they walked back to the mill. It was, Eleanor thought, a minor miracle that no one had tripped on the cobblestones, for it was clear few were paying attention to anything other than Brad's baby. And, based on the comments she overheard, the *Herald* was a beautiful, healthy baby.

Eleanor found herself counting the minutes until the workday ended and she could tell Brad how positive the reception was, and that she was far from the only one who'd chuckled with amusement over the articles he'd printed. Even though she'd read some of them as he'd been composing them, they lost none of their humor on the second reading.

When the final bell rang, Eleanor hurried out of the mill and looked for the familiar form, but Brad wasn't there. There were no lights on in the newspaper office, no sign of activity. Brad must be gone. *Of course he's gone. He has other things to do. He has other friends.* Eleanor tried to bite back her disappointment. It was foolish to be so upset. While it was true they'd developed a camaraderie, she needed to remember that Brad had his own life, and so did she. For tomorrow was the day she would begin her campaign for the mill workers' red clothing.

He's not an ogre, Eleanor told herself as she approached Charles Moreland's office the next day. Having learned that he took his dinner break after the mill workers', Eleanor had decided to forgo her own meal in order to meet him. *The worst he can do is refuse.* She continued her internal pep talk. *Remember all the times Papa told you how he'd convinced reluctant men to invest in his projects.* Eleanor had listened carefully, digesting business strategies along with roast beef and potatoes. Today she would see how much she had learned and whether she had inherited any of her father's persuasive skills.

"Is Mr. Moreland available?"

The mill owner's secretary looked as if this were the first time a worker had approached his boss. Perhaps it was. "Do you have an appointment?" he asked.

Eleanor shook her head. "No, sir, I do not. But I

won't take much of Mr. Moreland's time. Would you please tell him that Miss Eleanor Menger would like to discuss an opportunity to promote the mill?"

A minute later, the secretary ushered her into Charles Moreland's office. The man who controlled her fortunes and those of two hundred other mill workers rose to offer Eleanor a seat. "I don't believe we've met," he said when she had perched on the edge of the chair, reminding herself to breathe deeply. Surely that would cure her nervousness.

Eleanor studied the man she hoped to persuade to help her. He was tall, about the same height as Brad, but the resemblance ended there. While Brad's hair was auburn, this man's was blond, and his eyes were blue, not Brad's emerald green. The biggest difference was that Charles Moreland appeared at least five years older than Brad, though Eleanor had heard they'd been class-mates. What, she wondered, had caused the aging? Was it the fire that had killed his parents and injured one of his sisters? Perhaps it was the sabotage that had oc-curred at the mill last year. Perhaps it was his long-standing feud with Matt Wagner, the man who was now his brother-in-law. Eleanor didn't know the reason. She only hoped that past problems would not keep Charles Moreland from agreeing to her plan.

"I've been working in the weaving room for about a month," she explained.

The raised eyebrows gave him a haughty look. "And in a month you believe you've found a way to increase sales."

Eleanor shook her head. "My idea is for a new way to promote your products. As is true of most advertising, there is no guarantee of increased sales." Her father had expounded on that distinction several times.

"I see." Mr. Moreland was silent for a moment, his eyes appearing to assess her. "What is this idea?" he asked at last.

"The mill hands would like to march in the Independence Day parade. We want to be patriotic, so we'll wear blue and white clothing. What we need are red sashes." Before he could interrupt, Eleanor continued her explanation. "I was hoping that Moreland Mills would provide the fabric for those sashes."

His eyebrows rose again. "And how would this promote the mill?"

She had her answer ready. "We would carry a banner, made from the same red cotton, with 'Moreland Mills' embroidered on it. Furthermore, Brad—er, Mr. Harrod," Eleanor corrected herself, "Mr. Harrod will mention it in the *Herald*."

Charles Moreland's lips quirked in a smile, leaving a sinking sensation in Eleanor's stomach as she suspected he had noted and was amused by her slip. How embarrassing!

"I see." He nodded slowly. "You're very persuasive, Miss Menger." Though the words were positive, his tone remained neutral. Mr. Moreland reached for a sheaf of papers on the edge of his desk. Rifling through them, he extracted one. "Sheeting will probably drape better than toweling. Don't you agree, Miss Menger?"

Cautious optimism began to course through her veins. It sounded as if he would agree. "I can have five hundred yards dyed red," he said. "Will that be sufficient?"

Eleanor's heart sang with elation. "Oh, yes! Thank you." As she left the mill owner's office, Eleanor was smiling. Papa would be so proud.

"Never again." Charles clenched the silver candlestick so tightly his knuckles whitened. "I never want to go through this again."

Nor did Brad. In all the years he'd known Charles, he had never seen his friend so distressed. Perhaps a touch of humor would help. "I hate to point this out," Brad said, drawling his words, "but it's Susannah who's going through it. She's the one who's having a baby. All you have to do is wait."

"And that is the hardest thing I've ever done." Charles plunked the candlestick on the mantel with enough force to dent the marble. The two men were in Charles's study, the dark-paneled room where Brad had found the expectant father pacing the floor, his expression so grim Brad had initially thought both Susannah and the baby had died.

"I want to help her, but there's nothing I can do." Charles glared at Brad. "Stop smirking. When it's your turn, I can guarantee you won't be laughing."

"That assumes it ever will be my turn. I'm not placing any bets on that." Though he tried to keep his tone light, some of his wistfulness must have been obvious, for Charles's glare turned into a sympathetic smile.

"Nonsense! You just haven't met the right woman. When you do, you'll be married and a father before you know what's happened."

It sounded simple, but Brad knew better. He'd met hundreds of women. One of them had even refused his offer of marriage. But the only one who occupied his thoughts both night and day was a woman he could never marry. It was one thing to flout his parents' wishes and move out of Rose Walk. It was quite another to even consider marrying a mill worker. Brad had seen how Jane Moreland had been treated when she'd been engaged to Matt Wagner, even though Matt had risen far beyond his humble beginnings, and how the townspeople had scorned Matt for daring to love above his station.

It would be worse—much worse—for Eleanor if Brad started to court her. His parents would never agree, and without their sponsorship, the townspeople would shun her. That was a thought Brad could not bear. Eleanor was bright; she was beautiful; she was even bewitching. But she was not a woman he could marry, not unless he was willing to make both of their lives miserable.

"I've made a decision," he announced. "Just because you and Anthony didn't take our pact seriously doesn't mean that I don't." For the first time since Brad had arrived, Charles stopped pacing. "You two failed to honor our agreement," Brad continued. "You acted as if the decision not to marry young was of no consequence. I disagree, and so I've decided to show you how wrong you were. I shall never take a wife."

For a long moment, Charles stared at him. Then he

began to laugh. He laughed and laughed, and when he finally stopped, he had to wipe his eyes. "You're the best!" he announced. "You knew just what to say to get my mind off Susannah's ordeal."

It was Brad's turn to stare. Charles was mistaken if he thought Brad was joking. He wasn't. He was more serious than he'd ever been. It was useless, though, to try to explain that to his friend.

"How do your parents feel about the *Herald*'s success?" Charles asked when he'd resumed his pacing.

Why did Charles persist in raising topics he'd rather not discuss? "I wouldn't know," he said shortly. "I haven't seen Father since I moved out, and I suspect Mother is in a perpetual state of swoon over my living in a boardinghouse."

Charles sank into the leather wing chair opposite Brad. Once again his expression was serious, although the deep worry furrows were receding. "You need to mend the rift, Brad. You can't let it go on forever."

It hadn't been forever. "I'll admit I'm not happy about the situation, but I refuse to grovel to Father. He's the one who was wrong. He won't admit that I'm a responsible adult." And that stung, almost unbearably.

"Your father will come around. When everyone in town continues to sing your praises, he'll start taking credit for raising his son to be a shrewd businessman." Charles sounded confident.

It was a pleasing fantasy; unfortunately, Brad knew it was just that: a fantasy. "I wish I were as certain as you. Now, can we change the subject?"

"So long as it's not to my impending fatherhood."

"Fair enough. Let's talk about my favorite topic, the *Herald*."

"Is this a plea for more advertising?"

"Nope. You've already done enough. I've been considering having a column written by one of the mill workers. What do you think about that idea?"

A shadow crossed Charles's face. "That depends," he said. "I don't need another rabble-rouser. It's mighty galling to admit that the last person who stirred up trouble for me is now my brother-in-law."

And the man who'd won Jane's heart, causing her to refuse Brad's proposal. Brad blinked, surprised by the direction his thoughts had taken. It was odd to realize that he no longer felt anything but friendship for the woman he'd once wanted to marry. Perhaps Charles had been right when he'd claimed that Brad had never truly loved Jane. But love and marriage were not subjects he wanted to entertain. Not tonight. Not ever.

"I was thinking about the humorous aspects of mill life," he said.

Charles raised an eyebrow. "If you find any, let me know. Running a mill is serious business."

"True, but you must have lighter moments."

"You mean, like the time one of my weavers convinced me to donate hundreds of yards of fabric so she and the others could march in a parade?"

Brad heard heavy footsteps trudging up the stairs and hoped they didn't mean the doctor had been summoned. That couldn't be good news. Instead, he seized on Charles's last comment. "Eleanor didn't tell me you'd agreed."

The gleam in his friend's eye alerted Brad to his mistake. "You're on a first-name basis with her. Interesting. Very interesting."

There was no point in dissembling. Brad decided to try full disclosure. Maybe if Charles heard the whole story, he'd realize there was no reason to have that knowing smirk on his face. "Eleanor is the woman I met on the train, the one who preferred to read a newspaper rather than converse with me."

Charles's smirk widened. "And that, my friend, is even more interesting. As my wife might say, the painting has greater depth than I realized." He paused for a second. "Your Eleanor reminds me of someone, but . . ."

Before Charles could finish his sentence, a baby began to cry. Moments later, the midwife entered the study. "Mr. Moreland," she said, her face wreathed in a smile, "you have a son."

There was nothing unseemly about it. It wasn't as if this were an assignation or—even more shocking—a moonlight rendezvous. They were simply two people attending the same event. And, if they chose to sit together, well . . . there was nothing scandalous about it. Brad had come to report, while Eleanor was here in a show of support for her friend.

Though the Hidden Falls musicales were quarterly events, this was the first time Deborah had been asked to perform. The young woman, Eleanor knew from hearing her practice, had a lovely if untrained voice. Tonight she would be joining her alto in a duet with a soprano. Normally poised Deborah was so nervous over her debut that Virginia had agreed to remain backstage with her, leaving Eleanor alone. And so when Brad had asked if he might sit next to her, she had responded with a warm smile. An evening like this was far more enjoyable when it was shared with a friend. For though they stood at opposite ends of the Hidden Falls social scale, they were friends.

"You look lovelier than ever tonight." Brad's eyes moved slowly, as if he were considering each of her features, trying to decide what looked different.

"It's a new hairstyle," Eleanor told him. "Deborah's responsible." In addition to her bell-like voice, Deborah possessed an innate talent for styling hair. One of the first things Eleanor had noticed was that the two sisters were always perfectly coiffed. Today Deborah had declared that the best cure for her nervousness was to concentrate on something else, that something else being Eleanor's hair. The result was a chignon dressed low on Eleanor's neck instead of her normal Pompadour. The style was old-fashioned, reminding Eleanor of daguerreotypes she had seen of Mary Lincoln. It could have looked dowdy, but it did not. Somehow the formal style suited Eleanor.

"Your friend is a woman of many talents," Brad said, "like you."

"Me? What do you mean?"

Brad waited until a young family had taken the seats next to them before he replied. "I heard you convinced Charles to contribute to your cause." They'd agreed to refer to the parade as a cause whenever they might be overheard, since neither wanted to spoil the surprise. As he'd planned, Brad had begun introducing hints about a mysterious parade entry in the *Herald*. To his surprise and Eleanor's pleasure, the single-paragraph teasers had become one of the most talked-about sections of the paper.

"It wasn't difficult to convince him, once I explained the advantages." And once she'd overcome her nervousness. "Mr. Moreland is a sensible businessman."

Brad's eyes twinkled with amusement, as if he guessed how much courage she'd had to muster to approach his friend. "That may be true, but I heard you were extremely persuasive."

That was high praise, coming from someone as notoriously critical as Charles Moreland. "Then my father deserves the credit."

"Your father the shopkeeper." There was the slightest note of incredulity in Brad's voice, and Eleanor knew she'd made a mistake. The lessons her father had given her hadn't been based on his experiences running the haberdashery.

"If you're going to succeed, you need to persuade customers to buy goods they might not truly need," she said quickly. While that wasn't a lie, it wasn't the answer to Brad's question. Oh, how she hated these half-truths! Life would be so much simpler if she could admit she was the daughter of a wealthy financier. But simpler, Eleanor reminded herself, did not mean safer. Stories spread quickly, and one as unusual as an heiress working in a mill had the possibility of being disseminated far beyond the borders of Hidden Falls. That was a risk she could not take. But still she hated lying, especially to Brad, who'd told her how much he valued honesty.

In an attempt to change the subject, Eleanor looked around. The church, which served as the town's primary meeting place, was only two-thirds full. Both Brad and Virginia had mentioned that the musicales normally attracted a standing-room-only crowd.

"Do people usually come at the last minute?" Eleanor asked Brad. A surreptitious glance at her watch revealed five minutes until the performance was to begin.

He shook his head. "Everyone knows you need to get here early to be guaranteed a seat. I don't understand why there are so many empty places."

The only reason Eleanor could imagine was so unpleasant that she didn't want to voice it. Were the townspeople boycotting tonight's musicale because two of the mill hands would be performing? Surely not.

As several acquaintances passed, Brad rose and greeted them. When he was once more seated, he turned back to Eleanor. "I probably shouldn't ask this, but if your parents are as loving as they seem, I wonder why you left them."

It was a measure of Eleanor's distress that she found the subject of her parents easier to discuss than the empty pews. "My parents died," she said simply.

Brad's face clouded. "I am so sorry. I didn't mean to remind you of your loss."

"It happened eight years ago. The worst of the pain has subsided, but I still miss them every day. I'll find myself looking at something and wanting to tell one of them about it. Then I realize that I can't." Eleanor swallowed, trying to dissolve the lump that always settled in her throat when she thought of her parents. "I didn't realize how important my family was until I lost them."

Brad's lips quirked in the wry smile that never failed to touch her heart. "There are times I wish I could lose mine."

She shook her head. "Don't ever wish that."

"You sound like Charles. He said something similar."

"Perhaps that's because he's lost his parents too. 'Forever' and 'never' are a long time."

Brad's lips tightened. "You may be right, but let's talk of something more pleasant."

"Like the fact that you, who told me you are tone deaf and never go to concerts, are here?"

He chuckled. "You would have to mention that. No, I thought we'd talk about my favorite subject: the paper. I wondered if you'd write a column for the *Herald*."

"Me?"

"You. I think we need an article written about—and by—the mill workers. You're the perfect candidate."

"I thought you wanted a series of articles about initiations, featuring various groups."

"I do. This is in addition to that. The mill is the major employer in Hidden Falls. That makes you mill workers a large part of the population. It seems to me you're underrepresented, not to mention underappreciated. The column might be a way to change people's perceptions."

Eleanor couldn't fault his logic. He'd said nothing more than she'd thought on numerous occasions, the most recent being tonight. Though she wanted to believe otherwise, Eleanor knew it wasn't coincidence that this musicale would have a lower than normal attendance.

She voiced her greatest concern. "I don't know enough."

Brad shook his head. "I believe we've already discussed and dismissed that particular argument. And please don't tell me you're incapable of constructing a coherent English sentence. I've read your updates on the par . . . er, the cause, and they're good. Better than good, actually. You have a flair for writing."

"That's flattering, but I have no free time. The cause is taking every minute I'm not at the mill."

"You'll have more time when the cause is finished."

Brad had said she was persuasive. So was he, not to mention persistent. Eleanor nodded slowly. "I'll think about it then." Though she'd issued a disclaimer, she was tempted, very tempted. The truth was, she'd always enjoyed writing letters, and her mother had joked that Eleanor's diary was long enough to qualify as a novel. This would be similar and yet different. There'd be the same joy as she put words on paper, but being responsible for a column would provide new challenges. She'd have to find ideas that would interest the townspeople and a variety of ways to express those ideas. It would be hard work, but it could be fun.

The rest of the evening passed in a blur. Eleanor knew that Deborah's duet was well received and that the pianist's hands slipped twice during his performance, the resulting notes causing her to wince. She heard the people around her murmur appreciative comments. She saw Brad furiously scribbling notes. Though she was aware of all of those things, Eleanor felt as if she were observing them from a distance. While a small part of her was watching the performers, her brain whirled with the possibility of working on Brad's paper, and with each whirl, she grew more excited. Brad's suggestion had opened a door she hadn't realized existed. Writing the column would be a wonderful opportunity, not just for this year, but for the rest of her life.

When she had left New York City, Eleanor's only thoughts had been to avoid marrying Clifford Warren and to find a way to live until she received her inheritance. She had not thought beyond her twenty-fifth birthday. But even the short time she had been in Hidden Falls had made her realize that, no matter how much money she inherited, she had no desire to return to her life of leisure. Despite the cuts, blisters, and aching muscles, work at the mill provided more than wages. There was an undeniable satisfaction from being an active contributor to the town's economy.

Eleanor knew she did not want to remain at the mill for the rest of her life, but she also knew that needle-point and gardening would no longer satisfy her. She wanted to do something useful, something practical, something that had the power to change others' lives. Perhaps writing for a newspaper was that something. If she wrote the column Brad had suggested, she would have experience and credentials when she returned to New York.

As she accompanied Deborah and Virginia back to the boardinghouse, Eleanor said nothing about the possibility. Tonight was Deborah's night. She would do nothing to detract from that. But when the two sisters remained in the dining room, with Deborah accepting the other women's congratulations on her performance, Eleanor climbed the stairs to their room, more anxious than normal to begin her daily ritual of reading at least one newspaper.

The only place to read, she had discovered, was sitting on the floor directly underneath the gas lamp. She settled there and opened one of the newspapers she'd brought with her. Normally she read the out-of-town papers, looking for ideas she could share with Brad. She also scrutinized the New York City papers, hoping for a notice of Clifford Warren's marriage. Only then would she feel truly safe. Tonight she had another reason for reading, and that was to study other columnists' styles, analyzing what she liked and determining why some appealed to her more than others.

Perhaps half an hour had passed when Eleanor

turned a page and gasped. She read the short passage a second time and then a third, all the while trying to control the pounding of her heart. She hadn't imagined it. It was there in black and white. Instead of the announcement of Mr. Warren's nuptials, the paper bore a missing person notice. "Miss Eleanor Menger has disappeared," the announcement said. "Foul play is suspected. Anyone knowing of her whereabouts should contact Mr. Abel Kenton. A reward will be given for information leading to Miss Menger's return."

Eleanor shuddered, then dropped the paper as if it were burning her hands. She should have realized that Uncle Abel wouldn't give up easily and that when she did not return of her own accord, he would continue to seek her. The man was nothing if not determined, and for reasons known only to him, he had determined that she would marry Clifford Warren.

Forcing herself to take a deep breath, Eleanor exhaled slowly. Wasn't even breathing supposed to calm a person? She took another breath as she tried to convince herself she was safe. Uncle Abel would not find her, she told herself. Even though he had obviously enlisted others' aid, there was no reason he or anyone else would imagine she was in Hidden Falls. No one would expect her to be working in a textile mill.

Eleanor leaned against the wall and closed her eyes, trying to recall anything that would lead them here. Her name. Why hadn't she thought of that? She should have used an assumed one, but she hadn't, and now it was too late. Still, they had no way to trace her. She hadn't given her name when she'd purchased the railroad ticket, and the rolls at Moreland Mills were not public. Eleanor took another deep breath and exhaled. She was safe here. Of course she was.

Chapter Five

Eleanor couldn't help smiling. For once in her life, everything was going well. There had been heavy rain earlier in the week, causing a mild panic among the mill workers. What would they do if it rained on the big day? Would the parade be canceled? And, if it wasn't, would their beautiful new red sashes bleed all over their white blouses? But the rain had stopped yesterday morning, bringing a cloudless day that dried the ground. Today promised to be just as warm, a prospect that filled the marchers with glee. Independence Day, they announced, was supposed to be hot and dry.

"Just a little more to the left," Eleanor said as she adjusted one of the women's sashes. "Don't forget to smile," she admonished Millie and Virginia, who had been selected to lead the procession carrying the Moreland Mills banner. Though they would be the most visible, in Eleanor's estimation, Deborah would have the most demanding role, for she was to follow the banner, walking backward as she led the other women in song. Deborah had insisted she could maintain her balance and would not trip. Eleanor chose to believe her, though she doubted she herself could have managed the feat.

Deborah was probably right. For the past week, she'd been practically floating on air, buoyed by anticipation of going home to visit Franklin. Though the other women had teased her about knowing the exact number of hours until she'd see him again, Deborah hadn't minded. Their times to be just as excited were coming, she promised. But first there was the town's biggest annual celebration and its official introduction to the mill workers. That was just minutes away now.

Brad had arranged for the mill hands to be the last group marching in the parade. That, he had assured Eleanor, would only heighten the suspense. He claimed it also emphasized their importance, for everyone knew that the most favored entries were the first and last.

Eleanor was still amazed that no one appeared to have guessed the identity of the mysterious finale. With so many people involved in sewing sashes, designing and embroidering the banner, and rehearsing the songs they'd sing, it seemed nothing short of a miracle, but— though the town was buzzing with speculation—the predominant thought was that Brad's newspaper staff had constructed a float to be the culmination of the parade. Why else, people asked, would he feature it in the *Herald*?

Tradition decreed that the parade begin at the mill, travel up Rapids Street to Main, then follow Main back to Bridge, ending at the park. When Eleanor had learned that, she'd been pleased, for the route enabled the mill workers to gather inside the mill, remaining there until it was time for them to join the parade. No one would see them, but the large windows allowed them to watch the other celebrants.

"All right, ladies, smile for the camera." Brad's own smile was broad as he fastened his camera onto the tripod. "I want a picture of you getting ready to march." They had moved outside the mill and were preparing to join the parade.

When Brad gestured toward Eleanor, she shook her head. Though she told herself it was illogical, she could not dismiss the uneasiness she'd had since reading Uncle Abel's missing person notice. It was highly unlikely that he'd ever see a copy of the *Herald,* much less this particular issue, but she couldn't take the risk.

"Not me," she told Brad. "Millie and Virginia holding the banner is a better picture. If you center the banner, it'll make your friend Charles happy too."

Brad wrinkled his nose. "Oh, all right, but since you refuse to let your pretty face help me sell papers, you'll have to pay the penalty." The melodramatic tone he used for his final words told Eleanor she'd enjoy the penalty.

"What did you have in mind?"

"Two rides on the carousel."

She feigned horror before she agreed. "Only if those rides are on the ostriches."

"Were there other animals on the merry-go-round? I didn't notice." This was the Brad whose company she enjoyed so much, the one who was rarely without a smile.

As the women moved into marching formation, Eleanor took her place. Early on, she had decided that she'd position herself in the middle of the group but on one side. That way, if something appeared to be going amiss, she could move quickly to resolve it, but—by not being at the front—she would draw no undue attention to herself.

Here at the beginning of the parade route, there were fewer spectators than there would be on Main and Bridge Streets, but even with the smaller crowd, the comments were favorable. Eleanor saw smiles and heard *oohs* of pleasure as the women in their distinctive clothing joined the procession. They were marching slowly up the hill on Rapids Street when she overheard a middle-aged couple talking.

"Look, Jonathon, it's the mill girls." The woman sounded more than a little surprised.

"They're mighty purty," he answered, his voice booming.

From the corner of her eye, Eleanor saw the woman slap his arm playfully. "Jonathon, you're a married man!"

"But I ain't blind." She saw him grin. "Annie, honey, there ain't no harm in lookin'." If she hadn't been singing, Eleanor might have laughed along with him.

They were halfway down Main when Eleanor noticed two older women standing in front of the crowd. Both wore elaborate hats, one of which had a stuffed bird perched on the brim. Not to be outdone, the other woman had draped red-and-blue veiling over her white hat and had affixed a small flag to the center of the crown, turning herself into a human flag pole.

"Brad Harrod wasn't exaggerating when he said we'd be surprised," Bird Hat told her companion.

"It's a nice surprise, though," Flag Lady said. "In their red, white, and blue, those girls make me proud to be an American."

"I wonder why no one thought of it before."

"What do you mean? Lots of folks wear red, white, and blue." She gestured toward her hat, setting the flag to waving.

Bird Hat shook her head. "I meant the girls marching in the parade. I hadn't realized how many of them there were."

"Hundreds, I venture to say." Flag Lady appeared to be counting. "They have beautiful voices too. Now I'm sorry I missed the musicale."

The stuffed bird bobbled as the woman shook her head again. "You were the one who said she didn't want to listen to screeching." As Bird Hat pronounced the words, Eleanor realized she'd found a piece of the puzzle. At least some of the townspeople had boycotted the musicale, not out of disdain for the mill workers but because they'd doubted Deborah and the soprano's talents. Though the effect had been the same, the different motivation was more palatable.

"This is one time when I don't mind saying I was wrong." Though Flag Lady lowered her voice slightly,

Eleanor heard her add, "We ought to invite some of them to join the choir."

This was more than palatable. This was wonderful. A feeling of exultation swept through Eleanor. The choir, she had heard, was a bastion of respectability, organized by a group of the town's most influential women. Mill workers, Deborah had told her, were never included. The fact that Flag Lady and Bird Hat were even discussing inviting them was a major step forward. Eleanor heard her own voice, which was decidedly less melodious than Deborah's, soar with joy.

Half an hour later, the parade had ended and the women had removed their red sashes. Those and the banner would be carefully stored for next year's parade, for there was no doubt, based on the townspeople's reaction, that the mill workers would be regular participants.

"The girls were a success."

Eleanor turned to smile at Brad. She had seen him mingling with the crowd, interviewing some of the spectators, taking pictures of others. "Isn't it wonderful?" she asked. "They all look so proud."

"They should be. This really was a case of saving the best for last." Brad wrinkled his nose. "And now, Miss Menger, comes the worst part of the day, the speeches." He gestured toward the platform where a number of the town's dignitaries were already seated. "I'd escape if I could, but I need to cover this for the *Herald.* Those are my advertisers, you know."

In addition to the mayor and Mrs. McBride, Eleanor recognized Charles Moreland. The dark-haired woman next to him must be his wife. Judging from the resemblance, the blond on his other side was his sister Anne, which meant the handsome man next to her was her husband, carousel carver Rob Ludlow. Though there were a dozen other people on the platform, the only ones whose identities Eleanor could guess were a woman with hair the same shade as Brad's and a man whose square jaw and nose Brad had inherited.

Eleanor studied Brad's parents. Her own mother would have found Mrs. Harrod a kindred spirit, with elegant clothing and regal demeanor. Though his wife smiled freely, Mr. Harrod appeared more reserved, leading Eleanor to believe Brad's sense of humor had not come from this parent. His hair had. Though dark brown with distinguished silver wings at the temples, the unruly curls Mr. Harrod had obviously attempted to tame were part of his legacy to his son.

"I would be eternally grateful if you'd keep me company." That son was still speaking.

Eleanor pretended to consider his invitation. "I could be persuaded," she said slowly. "For a price, that is."

"Would that price be another carousel ride?"

"Precisely!"

"Agreed. Let's find a place to sit."

Eleanor had no way of knowing whether this was a larger than normal gathering, but the two sets of bleachers that provided good views of the platform were filled, leaving latecomers to either remain standing or sit on the ground. Some, it appeared, were prepared for the latter, for they'd brought old quilts with them.

Eleanor wondered where Brad expected them to sit. There were no longer any seats in the bleachers, and he had no blanket. Perhaps he recalled the day they'd met, when she'd sat on the grass, and assumed she wouldn't mind doing the same here. The truth was, she wouldn't mind, if she only had to consider herself. But today she wasn't simply Eleanor Menger. She was Eleanor Menger, one of the mill workers, and as such she had a reputation to maintain. If she wanted the townspeople to regard the mill hands as more than extensions of the machines and to realize that they were as genteel as Brad's mother, she needed to behave in a manner that was above reproof. A lady did not sit directly on the ground in a public place. Fortunately, Brad seemed to understand that, for he led her to a spot at one side of the bleachers. Here a handsome dark-haired man had spread a piece of oilcloth far too large for one person. When he saw Brad and Eleanor approaching, the man rose.

"Eleanor, may I present Reginald Jamison." Brad began the introductions. "Reginald is the single most important employee of the *Herald.* Reg, this is Miss Eleanor Menger."

Reg offered a self-deprecating smile. "Brad has been known to exaggerate. The only reason he thinks I'm so important is that I know how to clean type." Reginald's next smile changed its tenor. "He did not exaggerate your beauty."

Eleanor felt a flush rise to her cheeks. Brad had mentioned her to one of his employees, and he described her as beautiful. She couldn't help smiling. She wasn't beautiful, of course, but a girl didn't mind a gentleman thinking she was. She settled herself on the oilcloth, arranging her skirts to cover her shoes. There would be no feet—bare or otherwise—visible today. Today she would be the model of decorum.

Both Brad and Reg sat, and if Brad was close enough that she was aware of the scent of his soap, well, that didn't matter. A public gathering like this permitted greater proximity than might otherwise be acceptable.

As the mayor began his speech, Brad pulled out a piece of paper and began to take notes. Occasionally, though, he'd catch Eleanor's eye and either grin or wink, as if they were sharing a private joke. Indeed, she felt as if they were, for he held his pad so she could read the notes he was making, and some of them were decidedly irreverent. "Wind bag," Brad wrote as the mayor continued what seemed to be an interminable dissertation, quoting each president. Surely there was no need to recite the Gettysburg Address in its entirety, particularly when the mayor lacked Lincoln's eloquence. The rousing applause when Mayor McBride finished owed little, Eleanor suspected, to the content of his speech but more to the fact that it was over.

Brad's father, Charles Moreland, the town's attorney, even Rob Ludlow had been enlisted to "say a few words." Fortunately, at least from Eleanor's perspective, they limited themselves to no more than five minutes each. When the last dignitary on the platform had spoken and the mayor returned to the podium, Eleanor assumed he would announce that the ceremony would conclude with the singing of the national anthem. Instead, he looked around the audience, his gaze stopping when he reached Brad.

"Our final speaker will be Hidden Falls' newest entrepreneur. Ladies and gentlemen, please welcome Mr. Brad Harrod."

Eleanor blinked in surprise. Though they'd had numerous discussions of the day's events, not once had Brad mentioned that he would be one of the speakers. And if he was to deliver a speech, why hadn't he taken a seat on the platform?

Brad rose and walked to the podium. Less than two minutes later, he was once again standing at Eleanor's side, singing "The Star-Spangled Banner."

"That was another case of saving the best for last," she said softly when the music ended and the bleachers began to empty.

Brad raised an eyebrow. "The national anthem is always the finale."

Pursing her lips into the disapproving expression one of her teachers had perfected, Eleanor said, "You're choosing to misunderstand me. Your speech was wonderful, Brad." Unlike the others, it had stirred her heart and brought tears to her eyes.

"Come on," he said, placing her hand on his arm. "There are some people I want you to meet." Accepting the compliments of the people they passed, Brad led

Eleanor toward the back of the platform. There she saw Charles Moreland, his wife, and baby.

"So you're the woman who convinced my husband to donate the sashes," Susannah Moreland said when they'd been introduced. A strikingly beautiful brunet, she smiled at Eleanor, then glanced down at the infant she was holding. As she touched the baby's nose, her smile softened, giving her the appearance of one of the medieval Madonnas Eleanor had seen in art museums.

"The sashes turned out well, didn't they?" Brad directed the question to his friend.

Ignoring Brad, Charles smiled at Eleanor. "You were right. It was good advertising for the mill."

"It was exciting for us to be part of the celebration."

"We should have had the mill workers involved years ago." Brad laid his hand on top of Eleanor's and squeezed it gently.

"But if it was already a tradition, that wouldn't have helped you sell papers."

Brad's laugh rang out. "She won't let me forget that I'm mercenary."

"You're a prudent businessman," Eleanor countered.

Charles and Susannah exchanged a private glance before he clapped Brad on the shoulder. "If only Anthony could see you now! The final holdout is about to break the pact."

Brad's lips tightened, as if the reference annoyed him, and Eleanor felt his hand stiffen. Whoever this Anthony and the pact were, it was clear they were something Brad didn't want to discuss.

He turned toward Susannah and the baby. "So this is the boy who caused my friend so much distress. What's his name?"

"Louis," Susannah said. "Louis Deere Moreland. We named him after my father."

"The next one will be a girl," Charles announced. "We'll call her Brunhilda."

"Next one?" Brad appeared more surprised by the prospect of a second child than by the unlikely name. "I distinctly remember you telling me that you had sworn off children."

Charles and Susannah exchanged another one of those looks that told the world how much they loved each other. "That was then," Charles said, his eyes sparkling with mirth. "That was before I discovered how wonderful a child could be."

Brad's only response was an arched eyebrow.

"Would you like to hold Louis?"

Eleanor nodded as Susannah settled the baby in her arms. That was the courteous response. But courtesy had nothing to do with her reaction. She'd held children dozens of times before, but never before had it felt like this. Little Louis fit into the crook of her arm as if he had been made specially for it. He was warm and sweet, closing his eyes as if he were content to remain cradled in her arms for the rest of his life. And, oh how wonderful that was.

Eleanor closed her own eyes briefly, pretending it was her son she held. Never before had motherhood seemed so appealing. It was true, she had entertained dreams of a husband and children, but that had all been in the future. In her dreams, her husband's face had been blurred, and she'd never been able to picture herself with a child. Now she could. Now she could imagine herself sitting in a rocking chair, cradling a tiny boy, a boy with a square chin and a spattering of freckles on his cheeks, a boy who looked just like his father. Brad.

Eleanor's eyes flew open. How silly! She bent her face to the baby, hoping no one would notice her discomfort. What a ninny she was, imagining herself married to Brad Harrod. As Louis began to fuss, she handed him back to Susannah.

"Are you ready to ride the carousel?" Charles asked a moment later. "They're waiting for us."

To Eleanor's surprise, Brad looked at the people standing near the merry-go-round, then shook his head. "Perhaps in half an hour," he said, "when there's less of a crowd."

A quick glance at the queue told Eleanor Brad's concern was not the number of people in line but the identity of two of them. His parents stood at the head of the queue with the mayor and his wife. Eleanor imagined this would be a ceremonial ride, similar to the grand opening Deborah and Virginia had described. Once Charles and Susannah joined them, the Harrods and the McBrides as well as the day's other speakers would take one ride, then open the merry-go-round to the rest of the townspeople. Brad, it seemed, wanted no part of that ride, just as he had not wanted a seat on the platform. If Eleanor had had any doubts of the seriousness of the rift between Brad and his parents, his refusal to join them would have quenched those doubts.

"Have you seen Anne Moreland's nursery?" Brad asked when they'd left Charles and Susannah. Eleanor shook her head. "There's a tiny carousel, just the right size for children, in the back yard. Shall we go there?"

They walked for a few moments, her hand cradled in the crook of his arm, his hand resting on top of hers. There was nothing unseemly about it. Many couples walked this way. It was nothing more than a courteous gesture, and yet Eleanor could not deny the warmth that flowed through her as she felt Brad's hand press hers. Though a simple touch, the sensations it evoked were anything but simple. She felt safe, protected, and, oddly enough, cherished. All because this man was touching her hand.

And then, as the crowd thinned, he removed his hand from hers. In an instant, the warmth faded, and with it Eleanor's sense of well-being. Had she done something wrong? They'd been talking about the parade and the speeches, laughing at the inadvertently funny aspects of both. Surely nothing she had said would have given offense. While it was true they were no longer being jostled by others and she didn't need the support his hand provided, she'd enjoyed the feeling of closeness. That was gone. Though her hand remained on his arm, Eleanor felt as if she'd lost something precious and didn't know why. She couldn't ask. A lady wouldn't do such a thing. Instead, she'd continue walking as if nothing unexpected had occurred.

Brad had other ideas. Gently, he reached for her hand, removing it from his arm, and as he did, the blood drained from Eleanor's face. What was happening? Why was he rejecting her in such a public way? She took a step backward, wishing she could somehow disappear. *Ninny!* Eleanor told herself for the second time. *You're a ninny to read so much into a simple gesture.* But she couldn't help it.

And then, before she realized what he intended, Brad reached for the hand that now hung by her side, clasping it in his, threading his fingers through hers. Suddenly, the world was once again spinning on its axis. He hadn't rejected her. He didn't want to distance himself from her. Quite the contrary. Placing her hand on his arm as they walked had been a chivalrous gesture, one most gentlemen were taught at an early age. This was better—much, much better. No one was taught to hold hands as he and she were now. That was not a matter of etiquette or courtesy. It was an act of . . . Eleanor stumbled over the word. *Friendship?* Perhaps. Brad was certainly her friend. Eleanor hesitated as other words came to mind. *Affection. L . . .* No, she wouldn't even think that one. But surely there was no harm in letting herself believe just for a moment that there was more than friendship between them.

As Brad's fingers tightened on hers, waves of sensation chased rational thought away. Even through their gloves, Eleanor could feel the warmth of Brad's hand, his palm touching hers, his fingers meshing with hers as though they formed a single entity. Why had no one told her how lovely holding hands could be? Nothing had ever felt so wonderful.

If only the day would never end!

If only the day would never end! Though Brad had been attending Independence Day celebrations for his whole life, there had never been one like this. Never before had he been so aware of every detail; never before had he enjoyed even the simplest of events, like watching the color guard raise the flag; never before had he felt so completely alive. The reason wasn't hard to find. It was Eleanor who had changed everything. For the first time, he'd felt as if he were sharing the day with someone else, someone whose opinion he valued, someone who understood how he felt. Even those interminable speeches had seemed bearable, because she'd been there, sharing his boredom, somehow making even the mayor's pontification less stultifying.

They'd endured the speeches, but then they'd been set free. From the moment they'd left Charles and Susannah, everything had changed. It was if he'd adjusted his camera, bringing the world into focus. All his senses had been heightened, and he'd found himself acutely aware of a bird's trill and the pungent scent of crushed grass. Most of all, he'd been aware of Eleanor and the warmth of her hand on his arm. It had felt so good that he'd longed for more, and so he'd taken a chance, unsure of her reaction. The gamble had not backfired. By some miracle, Eleanor had not objected when he'd clasped her hand.

Had there ever been anything so glorious as walking toward the nursery, their hands entwined? Though there had been others bent on the same destination, Brad had felt as if he and Eleanor were in a world of their own, a magical world where anything was possible. And when they'd ridden the carousel, laughing as their ostriches began their stately up-and-down motion, he'd known a moment of pure joy, watching her smile. For the space of a ride, nothing had mattered but this woman who had somehow captured his heart. In that moment, Brad had felt like one of the knights of yore, vowing to protect his lady fair. No one would hurt Eleanor, not if he had anything to say about it.

When the day had begun, he'd thought his dream an impossible one, but with the passing of the hours, he'd seen glimmers of hope that a future with Eleanor might be possible. First there had been the time they'd spent with Charles and Susannah. Brad had watched them carefully, looking for signs of disdain, but he'd seen none. His friends had accepted Eleanor for what she was: a lovely, intelligent woman. The fact that she worked at Charles's mill didn't matter. They saw her as Eleanor, nothing more, nothing less.

The townspeople were a higher hurdle. Brad knew that. But today had seemed like a beginning, and an auspicious one at that. He had not imagined the favorable comments he'd heard as the mill workers had marched, nor the way the townspeople had greeted the standard-bearers, Virginia and Millie. He'd seen the smiles and overheard the praise when Deborah's clear alto had blended with a hundred other voices. Today they'd been a town, united in a single purpose: celebrating their country's independence.

It was possible the glow might fade. Brad was realistic enough to know that. It was possible the town would return to its former disdain of the mill workers, and Brad would have no choice but to defend the woman he loved. Fortunately, he possessed something the medieval knights had not: the power of the press. He'd use it and every other weapon in his arsenal to protect Eleanor from the townspeople's slights and slings.

As they descended from the carousel, Brad pulled out his watch, frowning when it confirmed what his stomach had been announcing, namely that it was time for dinner. Why hadn't he thought about food? He couldn't recall whether Mrs. Larimer had said she would be serving dinner and supper today. He suspected she and the other housemothers were taking a much-deserved holiday, for many of the mill hands were seated on quilts, pulling food from cloth bags.

"Are you hungry?" Eleanor asked. So much for subtlety. His concerns had not gone unnoticed. When he nodded, she smiled. "Mrs. Weld cooked extra yesterday so we could all pack bags for today. Would you like to share my dinner? I have much more than I can eat."

A few minutes later, they were seated on Reginald's oilcloth. As soon as they'd arrived, Reg had declared a burning desire to ride the merry-go-round. Good man. Brad would have to give him a raise. Somehow he'd realized that Brad wanted to be alone with Eleanor—as alone as they could be, surrounded by the majority of Hidden Falls. Perhaps it was his imagination, but Eleanor's smile made him think she felt the same way.

To Brad's surprise, she pulled two tin plates from her sack and began arranging food on them. Two plates? His spirits soared at the thought that she'd planned for them to dine together. Had there ever been such a wonderful, thoughtful woman?

"This has been the best Independence Day I can recall," he said after he'd taken a long swallow of lemonade. Though they were sitting in the park, surrounded by hundreds of Hidden Falls citizens, Brad's imagination conjured the picture of Eleanor on the opposite side of the table from him, three times a day, every day.

"It was pleasant, wasn't it?" She offered him another piece of fried chicken.

"It was far more than pleasant," he countered. Wonderful, exhilarating, unforgettable. Those were adjectives he'd use to describe the day. "I wouldn't change a single minute, except—of course—for those boring speeches."

She flashed him a wry smile. "Be careful, Brad. You were one of those speakers."

"I was including myself in the category of entertainment that should have been eliminated."

"You're wrong, you know. Even if most of them were too long, the speeches were important. They helped remind us of the reason we were celebrating." She swallowed a bite of biscuit before she smiled again and said, "Yours was the best."

The warmth of her voice made him want to smile. Instead, Brad muttered, "Because it was the shortest."

She shook her head. "That's false modesty, Brad. You captured the spirit of the day. I hope you're planning to print your speech in the next *Herald*."

The thought appalled him. "I can't do that."

"Why not?"

"Because it would be self-aggrandizing."

Eleanor shook her head again. "You can include excerpts from the other speeches too. Create a commemorative edition. Everybody will want one, and you'll sell more papers."

"Ouch! You won't let me forget that, will you?"

"Of course not. I want you to succeed."

That was what Brad wanted too, but suddenly the success he sought had nothing to do with the *Herald*'s revenue. Charles would laugh; in fact, he'd probably gloat. Anthony would be just as bad. So what? Brad didn't care if they both said, "I told you so." Though it had been only a short while since he'd declared himself a candidate for permanent bachelorhood, Brad knew how foolish that statement had been—as unrealistic as the pact he and his friends had made to delay marriage until their thirtieth birthdays. Charles had been correct when he'd prophesied that Brad would change his mind. He had, and sooner than anyone might have predicted. The reason was sitting next to him, sipping the last of the lemonade.

This was hardly a romantic setting. Perhaps he should wait. But he couldn't. He needed to know whether he had a chance at happiness. Brad swallowed deeply, mustering every ounce of courage he possessed. Though he was skilled at putting words on paper, this was far more difficult. He swallowed again, saying a silent prayer for eloquence. "If your father were alive, I'd be having this discussion with him."

As Eleanor's eyes widened, Brad realized she had no inkling of his thoughts. Though they'd laughed together, held hands, and shared a meal, it was a long way from holding hands to what he was about to propose. How would she react? Would she scoff at the idea or welcome it? There was only one way to know. "I'm not sure of the proper protocol, but . . . well . . ." Brad paused, searching for the right words. Finally he blurted, "I would like to court you."

Her green eyes widened again, and he saw the confusion in them. He'd been too precipitous. He should have waited until he had found a way to signal his wishes before he actually voiced them.

"Oh, Brad!" There was a hint of wonder in her voice. Surely that was a good sign.

"Does that mean yes?"

She shook her head ever so slightly. "It means that you surprised me."

He should have waited, but he hadn't and so he needed to help her understand how he felt. "This may seem sudden, because we've known each other less than two months, but I can't get you out of my mind." The furrows between her eyes were not a good sign. Oh, why did words fail him now? "You're the best thing that's ever happened to me, Eleanor. You understand me; you inspire me; you make me laugh. That's why I want you to be part of my life forever."

Though the furrows eased, her expression remained serious. Eleanor reached forward and laid a hand on his. As if realizing what she'd done, she snatched it back. "You're right," she said slowly. "This does seem sudden."

"But you care for me, don't you?" He couldn't believe he'd been mistaken about that.

She nodded. "I enjoy your company very much, and I want to be your friend, but I can't encourage you to consider anything more. I'd be all wrong for you."

Though she hadn't pronounced the words, she was clearly thinking of the fact that she was a mill worker, while his father was one of the wealthiest men in Hidden Falls. Brad wouldn't tell her that didn't matter to him. It didn't, but somehow he knew that argument would not convince Eleanor. Instead, he said, "Let me be the judge of that. I think you're perfect for me."

Her eyes darkened. "Oh, Brad, I'm far from perfect for you or anyone. Please, let's not destroy our friendship. Can't we go back to being friends?"

Friends! That wasn't what he wanted. It wasn't enough. He wanted the happiness Charles and Susannah shared, the joy Anthony had found with his Gracie. But that happiness continued to elude Brad. "What's wrong with me?" he asked, trying to keep the frustration out of his voice. "First Jane, now you. No one wants to marry me."

Eleanor was silent for so long that Brad feared she would not answer him. At last she said, "I don't know Jane, so I can't speak for her, but I do know that I'm not ready for marriage to you or anyone else. The truth is, I don't believe you're ready either."

She was wrong, totally and completely wrong.

"Please, Brad," she continued, "let's be friends. If you feel the same way in a year, we can talk about courting then."

"A year! That sounds like forever."

"It's not forever, and in the meantime, we'll have our friendship. Please." Eleanor extended her hand for the shake that would seal their bargain. He looked at it for a second, then took it in his and raised it to his lips. Pressing a kiss on her palm, Brad vowed that no matter what Eleanor said, he would not wait a year. She was the woman he loved, and he was going to marry her. Soon.

Brad was in his office the next day when Reginald announced that he had a visitor, two in fact. "Your parents," Reg muttered. It was the first time the elder Harrods had come to the newspaper, and for the briefest of moments, Brad entertained the hope that they were here to congratulate him on the paper's success. One look at their faces destroyed that illusion.

"So this is where you work." Father walked around the small room Brad used as an editorial office, touching nothing but obviously evaluating each piece of furniture and equipment.

"You need a tall plant in that corner," his mother

said. "A few paintings on the wall, maybe a rug." Unlike Father, she took one of the chairs he'd pulled out for them and continued to look around the room. His survey complete, Father stood next to her, resting a hand on her shoulder.

Brad tried not to sigh. "I don't imagine you came here to discuss my décor."

"No, we did not." Though Father remained standing, Brad settled behind his desk. The inevitable criticism might be easier to swallow if he were seated. "What I predicted has happened," his father continued. "You've made us the laughingstock of Hidden Falls."

No one could ever accuse Jacob Harrod of pulling his punches. Brad took a deep breath and tried to keep his voice calm. "Just how did I manage that? The *Herald* is doing well. Our sales, advertising, and the overall reception have been greater than I dared hope."

"That's not the problem. It's a better caliber paper than I'd expected."

Brad leaned back in his chair. "I'll accept that as a compliment, no matter how grudging it might be."

His father bristled. "There's no need to take that tone with me, my boy, not when you've humiliated your mother and me."

Now they were getting to the crux of the matter, the reason for the visit. "How were you humiliated?"

"That girl!" Father spat the words as if they had left a sour taste in his mouth. "Did you think no one would notice that you spent most of yesterday with her? You rode the carousel not once but three times, and you shared her supper. You were even seen holding her hand."

Brad clenched his fists, then slowly released them. This was a scene that had been repeated numerous times. Though the setting and the subject were different, the message was the same. Brad Harrod had failed to meet his father's expectations.

"Your reports are accurate," he said in the calm voice that he knew from experience irritated his father more than a shouted response would.

"How could you, Brad?" For the first time, his mother joined the fray. In the past, she would retire to a distant part of the house while his father berated him. "How could you think we'd approve of you seeing a mill hand?"

Brad kept his voice gentle as he turned to his mother. "That mill hand is a beautiful, charming, intelligent woman."

"She's a common laborer." Father's voice rose ten decibels.

"So am I." Brad held up his hands. "These ink stains are the result of honest hard work. I want you to know that I'm proud of them, just as I'm proud of what Eleanor does."

His parents exchanged glances before his father took a step toward the desk. "I realize this girl is only a passing fancy," he said, his voice lower than before. "But this must stop *now.*"

"That sounds like an ultimatum." There was always one, normally a threat to withhold Brad's allowance.

Father nodded. "I had hoped it wouldn't come to this, but if you persist in seeing that girl . . ."

"Her name is Eleanor."

"That girl," Father repeated. "If you persist in this foolishness, I will have no choice but to disown you. You and that girl will not inherit one penny from me."

"And you think that will deter me?" Had his father learned nothing about Brad? Though it was the first time Father had employed this particular threat, he should have remembered that threatening Brad only made him more determined to continue his course of action. "Don't you see, Father? I don't care about your money. You can threaten me all you want, but it won't change anything. I plan to live my life the way I see fit. And that includes Eleanor, if she'll have me."

His father glared, waiting for Brad to drop his gaze. When Brad did not, he sighed. "Come, Mae." Father reached for his wife's hand. "Your son has made it clear that he doesn't care about us."

But he did. Oh, how he did! The money didn't matter. Since he'd moved into the boardinghouse, Brad had learned that he could live with surprisingly few material possessions. But he wanted his parents' approval, and—more than that—he wanted their love. Sadly, it seemed he had neither.

Chapter Six

Every bone in her body ached. Eleanor could not recall when she had felt so ill. Chills alternated with fever, leaving her with limbs so weak the only way she could walk was if both Deborah and Virginia supported her, and even then she could manage no more than a few steps.

"You cannot go to the mill today." The first bell of the day had rung. Though Eleanor suspected neither Virginia nor Deborah had slept much last night, listening to her fevered tossing, Virginia's voice was as cheerful as if she'd wakened fully rested.

"I need to." Eleanor hated the way her words came out as little more than a croak. Virginia might be matter-of-fact about it, but Eleanor could not afford to miss a day of work. So far she had saved no money. Her pay as an apprentice was less than a fully trained mill worker's, and it had taken every penny to pay for a change of clothing. Perhaps in another month, she could afford a day without pay, but not now. She had no choice; she had to work.

Deborah splashed water on her face, then looked at Eleanor as she patted herself dry. "It'll only be for a day or two," she said.

"I don't know, Deborah." Virginia placed a cool hand on Eleanor's forehead. "She looks mighty sick. I think we better call Dr. Kellogg."

"No." Doctors cost money, and that was one thing Eleanor did not have. Dimly, she realized how far she had come from her sheltered life in New York. While her parents had been alive, she had never worried about money. The one time she'd injured herself, breaking her ankle while ice skating, her mother had summoned the physician. Though he'd made numerous house calls, not once had either of Eleanor's parents mentioned the cost. Now, the thought of one doctor's visit made Eleanor shiver more than the fever.

As if she had read Eleanor's thoughts, Deborah knelt by her side and patted her hand. "Don't worry about anything. The important thing is to recover your health."

Someone must have called Dr. Kellogg, for a few hours later, Mrs. Weld led him into Eleanor's room. "It's the grippe," Eleanor heard him say when he'd concluded his examination. "There's nothing to do but let it run its course. I've given her something to make her sleep."

Eleanor lost all sense of time. Dimly, she was aware

of Virginia and Deborah coming into the room. They must have slept there. Perhaps they spoke to her, but that might have been only a dream. She had vague memories of someone offering her cool water and a soothing broth. Perhaps that was Mrs. Weld. Mostly she slept.

"You're looking better today."

Eleanor opened her eyes and pulled herself to a sitting position. For the first time, her head did not feel as if it were spinning. She looked at the tray of food Mrs. Weld was carrying and realized she was hungry.

"I imagine you'll be able to come downstairs tomorrow," the housekeeper continued. "You wouldn't want to miss my creamed spinach."

Eleanor blinked in confusion. Creamed spinach was part of Mrs. Weld's special Sunday meal. "What day is it?"

"Why, today's Saturday." The housekeeper's face radiated friendly concern. "You took ill Tuesday night."

The fog surrounding Eleanor began to recede. Saturday. That meant she had missed four days of work. She tried not to wince as she did a mental calculation of lost wages. Vaguely, she recalled the doctor's visit. Had he been here more than once? How would she pay him?

Eleanor's mind began to whirl. Four days. She hadn't seen Brad since the Independence Day celebration. In her fevered state, she'd replayed portions of their last discussion, when he'd asked permission to court her. At the time she'd refused, it had seemed the correct—the only possible—response. But as her body had battled the illness, she'd been haunted by the fear that she'd made a mistake in not explaining her reasons. Did Brad understand her concerns? She couldn't let him endure the same shunning by the townspeople that Jane Moreland had experienced during her engagement to Matt Wagner.

Brad's question had been so unexpected that Eleanor had reacted without thinking, and in doing so, she might have hurt him. He deserved an explanation, but four long days had passed with her being unable to provide it. And even now, though she longed to see him and to somehow ensure she had not injured his pride, she could not move from this bed.

Eleanor frowned as she wondered how long it would be until she was back to work and able to see Brad again. Today was Saturday . . . Saturday? Eleanor's eyes fell on the bed the Sempert sisters shared. Surely she'd heard both of them preparing for work this morning, but that made no sense.

"Was Deborah here this morning?" she asked. When Mrs. Weld nodded, Eleanor shook her head in dismay. "She was supposed to be going home to see her beau." For weeks, her impending trip to the family's farm had been Deborah's favorite subject. She'd talked about how much she missed her parents, and her face had worn a soft glow when she'd spoken of Franklin, her intended. Deborah was to leave on the last train Friday night, returning ten days later. But for some reason, she had not.

"I reckon Deborah postponed her trip." Mrs. Weld placed the tray in front of Eleanor, uncovering a bowl of delicious-smelling soup. "She and Virginia are mighty tired these days, workin' an extra loom."

Though she longed to assuage her hunger pangs, Eleanor's hand paused, the spoon of chicken soup halfway to her mouth. "An extra loom? I don't understand."

Mrs. Weld settled on the bed opposite Eleanor. "You didn't think Mr. Greeley would let your loom sit idle while you were sick, did you?"

"No, of course not." Nothing kept the looms idle. "I thought one of the apprentices would run it."

"But then you wouldn't get paid."

Eleanor felt her eyes widen in surprise. "You mean Deborah and Virginia did extra work so I wouldn't lose my wages?"

Mrs. Weld shrugged, as if the answer should be apparent. "They're your friends, aren't they?"

Indeed, they were. Probably the best friends Eleanor had ever had. Though she counted numerous women as friends, both at school and at home, she could not imagine one of them being so generous. These women, women her own mother would have disdained for their humble background and lack of education, had redefined the word *friendship*.

When she'd finished the soup and leaned back in bed, Eleanor found her mind whirling. The Sempert sisters had done so much for her. If only there were something she could do to repay them.

"I don't know how to thank you for all you've done," Eleanor told them when they returned to their room that evening. Though she'd slept most of the afternoon, she had wakened with her head clearer than it had been in days. Two things had been apparent: She needed to make things right with Brad, and she had to find a way to show Deborah and Virginia how much she appreciated their friendship.

The sisters shrugged, as if their efforts had been trivial. "No thanks are necessary," Virginia said. "You'd have done the same for us."

They were underestimating the value of their gift. It was true Eleanor would have helped them if they'd asked. But Virginia and Deborah had done far more than that. They'd anticipated her need and resolved her problem without being asked. No one else Eleanor knew would have been so thoughtful or so generous. "I still don't know how to thank you, especially since you gave up your time with Franklin." Eleanor directed the final comment at Deborah.

"I'll go home next month." A wry smile crossed the brunet's face. "If what they say about absence making the heart grow fonder is true, Franklin will be very fond of me by then."

Later that evening, Eleanor posed the question she'd been pondering all day. As the sisters prepared for bed, she asked as casually as she could, "If someone gave you a large sum of money, what would you do with it?"

"That's easy." Virginia was the first to respond. "I'd buy every book I could." She paused, looking out the window for a second. "No, maybe I wouldn't do that.

Instead, I'd go to New York or Boston or Philadelphia so I could listen to those lectures I've read so much about. I wouldn't need to buy books there. I could use the libraries."

Deborah smiled at her sister. "You'd be able to go to the best normal school in the country," she pointed out, reminding Eleanor that Virginia dreamed of becoming a teacher.

"What about you, Deborah?" Eleanor asked. "What would you do?"

"I'd take singing lessons." She shrugged as if it were of no import, though the expression in her eyes said otherwise. "That's just a dream. We have no rich relatives to leave us an inheritance."

Perhaps not, but in less than a year, they would have a friend whose inheritance could help make dreams come true. And, in the meantime, the same friend had two ideas for turning at least a portion of those dreams into reality.

"What's got your socks all twisted?" Unable to concentrate on his work, Brad had come to the mill, hoping some time with Charles would clear his mind. His friend had taken one look at his face and closed the door behind them, perching on the edge of the desk while Brad slumped in a chair.

"I hadn't realized it was that obvious." There was no point in equivocating. "My parents paid me a visit a couple days ago."

"Your expression says it wasn't a pleasant visit."

"That's an understatement, if there ever was one. Father threatened to disown me if I persist in what he considers my reprehensible behavior."

"The *Herald*?" There was no mistaking Charles's concern. He knew how important the paper was to Brad.

If only it were that simple. "Surprisingly, no. Father's found something else that irks him even more— my friendship with Eleanor."

"Has he ever met her?"

"Of course not." That was part of the problem, but Brad had no idea how to resolve it. "You know the importance my parents place on social standing."

Charles nodded. "Mine were the same way, although my father relented in the end and agreed that Matt could court Jane." Though Charles wrinkled his nose at the thought of his new brother-in-law, the wry expression turned to a grin, as if were about to reveal a pleasant secret. "Susannah was quite taken with Eleanor. I gather they talked about art museums, and now she wants to ask Eleanor's opinion about the painting she's working on."

It was a high honor. Brad knew that Susannah, like many artists, preferred no one see her work until it was completed. Even Charles was rarely invited to comment on a painting in progress.

"Your wife has excellent taste in people, except for husbands, that is."

Though Brad thought his tone conveyed irony, Charles's response was more serious than he'd expected. "Do you think she should have married Anthony?" Before she'd met Charles, Susannah had been engaged to their friend Anthony for a brief period.

"Absolutely not! You know I was only joking. Anyone with even half an eye can see you're perfect for each other. And, judging from Anthony's letters, Gracie is perfect for him."

"She was."

"Was?" Brad reacted to Charles's suddenly solemn expression as well as the past tense of the verb. "What do you mean?"

Charles gestured toward a pile of papers on his desk. "I received a letter from Anthony today. Gracie died somewhere in France. He didn't say much else other than that he's coming back to the States."

"How awful!" Brad closed his eyes, imagining the anguish his friend was enduring. Though still unmarried, Brad shuddered at the thought of losing a beloved wife. This week had seemed interminable, filled with deep foreboding. The reason hadn't been hard to find. It wasn't because of the confrontation with his parents. As unpleasant as that had been, it hadn't caused him to lose sleep. But when he'd learned that Eleanor was ill, Brad's imagination had conjured a host of possibilities, each more dire than the preceding. People didn't die of the grippe, he told himself, though he knew that was not always true. Still, he'd lain awake at night, thinking of a world without Eleanor and hating the prospect. How much worse would it have been if they'd been married, and he'd grown accustomed to having her share his life? Poor Anthony!

Charles nodded. "Anthony's letter was a painful reminder that life can be short." He paused for a second,
weighing his words. "I know I've said it before, but I'm
not sure you listened to me. Don't let this rift with your
parents continue, Brad. You may think there's time to
repair it, but there may not be."

Charles picked up a paperweight, his grip so tight his
knuckles whitened. "I said things to my father that I'd
give anything to retract, but I can't. He died before I
could tell him I was wrong." Charles stared at Brad, his
expression more serious than Brad had ever seen.
"Don't let that happen to you."

"I don't want the rift to be permanent, but I won't
stop seeing Eleanor." This week had shown him just
how important she was to his happiness.

"There has to be a way to compromise."

Brad frowned. Charles made it sound easy when it
wasn't. "I wish I could find one." As painful as it was to
admit it, so far, that was one more failure for Brad.

"It's good to see you again. I was worried about you."

Today was Eleanor's first day back at work. Though
every muscle ached and she was more exhausted than
she'd been in weeks, her heart sang with pleasure at
Brad's words, and her feet, which had felt as if they'd
been weighted with grindstones, practically danced as
she hurried toward him. She'd spotted him the instant
she'd emerged from the mill. He'd been standing near the
newspaper office, his face lighting with a smile when
he saw her. Eleanor suspected her own smile matched

his. She had so much she wanted to say to him, but for a moment, all she could do was stare at him, cataloging each of his features, convincing herself he'd not changed during their week apart, that her refusal of his courtship hadn't hurt him.

"Dr. Kellogg said I had a particularly bad case of the grippe." She had dozens of things to tell him, and yet the first words that came out of her mouth were mundane.

Furrows appeared between Brad's eyes as he drew her away from the crowd. Though still inside the mill grounds, here their conversation would not be overheard. "Should you be back to work so soon?"

The very sinews of her body shrieked "no," but Eleanor said, "I can't expect Virginia and Deborah to do my work forever." She shook her head slowly. "Did you know that's what some of the mill hands do? They take on a sick girl's looms so she won't lose her wages." Eleanor wasn't certain how anyone could run three looms. She'd yet to master two. "I cannot believe they did that and won't accept any payment."

Brad didn't seem surprised. "Friends help each other. They're true friends."

Just as Brad was her friend. Or possibly more. It was the perfect introduction to her proposal. "I want to do something for them, and for the other mill workers too."

When Brad raised an eyebrow, encouraging her to continue, Eleanor said, "I've had a lot of time to think." That was the only positive aspect to being bedridden. She'd thought of Deborah and Virginia's generosity and her own desire to help them. She'd thought of

Brad's request to court her and his obvious disappointment at the prospect of mere friendship. She'd thought of his wish for a column in the *Herald* devoted to the mill workers and what that might mean for her future. Perhaps there was a way to address all of those wishes.

"Have you heard of the Lyceum Movement?" she asked. Using the Greek model developed by Aristotle so many centuries earlier, the lyceum sought to provide lectures and concerts to educate as well as entertain the public.

Brad wrinkled his nose as he did whenever he tried to recall a fact. It was, Eleanor thought, one of his most endearing expressions, for it gave him the appearance of an earnest schoolboy. "Vaguely. Wasn't that popular in Boston in the thirties?"

Eleanor nodded. "They had one in Lowell too." Lowell, Massachusetts had been one of the most progressive textile factory towns, serving as a model for the rest of the country. When he'd founded Moreland Mills, Charles Moreland's grandfather had incorporated many of the practices he'd seen in Lowell. Whenever possible, he'd improved them. He had not, however, introduced a lyceum. "From everything I've read, the Lowell lyceum was a wonderful experience for the mill workers."

The sparkle in his eyes and the crooked smile told Eleanor Brad knew where she was heading. "Shall I assume you believe Hidden Falls should have its own lyceum?" he asked.

She nodded again. "The more I thought about it, the

more it made sense to me." Eleanor told Brad about Virginia and Deborah's desire for higher education and cultural events and how the lyceum would satisfy them. "What do you think of the concept?"

Brad was silent for a moment, the furrows between his eyes telling her he was weighing the idea carefully. "I like it," he said at last. "I know you intend the lyceum for the mill workers, but it would benefit everyone in Hidden Falls, not just your friends."

Though she agreed with Brad, the tone of his voice concerned Eleanor. "Why do I sense that your next word was going to be 'but'?"

He grinned. "Because your instincts are accurate. It's a good idea. Actually, it's an excellent idea, but"—he paused for emphasis—"it will take a lot of work to establish a lyceum."

Eleanor had considered that. "I thought we could begin on a small scale."

"We?" There was no mistaking Brad's amusement.

"I was hoping you'd help."

His mouth quirked in a wry smile. "I will . . . for a price."

"Another carousel ride?"

"The price is a lot higher than that." Brad placed her hand on his arm and started walking toward their boardinghouses. "I'll do what I can. I can persuade some speakers to come here. I'll find us a place to hold the lectures. I'll even promote the lyceum in the *Herald.* I'll do all that if you agree to write a column for me."

"That's all?"

Brad raised both eyebrows. "What do you mean, is that all? You never agreed to the column."

"I'm agreeing now." During part of her enforced bed rest, she'd considered how much could be gained by writing the series of articles he'd proposed. "When do you want the first one, and how long should it be?"

As they discussed the timing and content of Eleanor's column, she felt her excitement rise. As Brad had said, the lyceum would be good for everyone in Hidden Falls. Her column could have similar benefits, breaking down barriers, helping the townspeople to understand and appreciate the mill workers. The possibility of good coming from those endeavors was wonderful. But so too was the fact that she'd have two reasons to spend more time with Brad. Her friend.

Chapter Seven

"I think it's a wonderful idea, and you're the perfect person to do it." The smile that accompanied Virginia's words left no doubt of her sincerity. Eleanor had wondered what her friends would say when she told them about Brad's proposal. His proposal that she write a column for the *Herald,* that is. Eleanor had no intention of telling anyone, not even her closest friends, about Brad's other proposal. That was a memory she savored in her quiet moments, guarding it as carefully as she did the few treasures she'd brought with her. But the paper was different. She wanted to know her friends' opinion. Still, conscious they might disapprove, Eleanor had waited until the three of them were alone in their room before she mentioned that she'd be writing a column for the *Herald.* She need not have worried.

"Virginia's right," Deborah chimed in. Though she'd

been giving her hair its hundred-stroke brushing, the
first part of which involved bending down so that blood
rushed to her scalp, she stood up as she added, "I don't
know of anyone else who could do it better. You have a
real way with words." Deborah resumed the brushing.
"I can't thank you enough for what you wrote to
Franklin. When he reads that, he'll surely stop being
miffed that I wasn't able to come home."

"It was the least I could do." As badly as Eleanor had
felt that Deborah had had to postpone her trip home, her
guilt had increased when she'd learned that Franklin
seemed in an ill humor over the delay. Deborah had
been distraught, and so Eleanor had volunteered to write
a letter to Franklin, explaining how Deborah had sacrificed her own pleasure to ensure Eleanor did not lose
wages. Though she'd stopped short of saying that such
unselfishness would make Deborah an ideal wife for
Franklin, Eleanor had crafted the letter so that Franklin
could take pride in his future bride's generosity.

"What will the column be about?" Deborah asked.

Eleanor reached for the button hook and began to un-
fasten her shoes. "Brad wants stories, what he calls
amusing anecdotes, about mill life. Our goal is to help
everyone in town understand what it's like to work at
Moreland Mills."

The instant the words were out of her mouth, Eleanor
realized her mistake. Had Virginia and Deborah noticed
her use of the plural pronoun? It was Brad's paper,
Brad's plan. She'd made it sound as if they were part-
ners, when they were . . . friends. A quick glance

showed no change in the sisters' expression. They must not have noticed her slip.

"If I'm right, it won't be only Hidden Falls residents who read your column." Virginia's voice rang with certainty. "I wouldn't be surprised if your stories become so popular that the city papers carry them too."

Eleanor shook her head at the suggestion. Though it was true that some columns were reprinted by other papers, she wasn't vain enough to believe that would happen to hers. "That's about as likely to happen as the Hudson River flowing north."

Deborah looked up again. "You say that a lot. I've always wondered what you meant by it," she admitted. "Is it the same as once in a blue moon—not very often?"

"I think Eleanor means never," her sister suggested.

"Exactly." It had been a private family game, finding unusual ways to say never. Papa would announce, "When bridges reach to heaven," while Mama's preferred phrase was "When mules fly." Eleanor, who'd been studying geography at the time, had chosen the river's inexorable descent to the sea.

She smiled at the sisters as she said, "Brad would be thrilled if the paper had a wider circulation, but he doesn't expect that to happen. The *Herald*'s appeal is local."

Her hair crackling with electricity from all the brushing, Deborah tried to smoothe it with her hands. "I just know you're going to be a famous newspaper writer someday, and everyone will envy me when I tell them you're my friend."

Eleanor smiled again. "It's a nice idea." She wouldn't deny the appeal of having people appreciate her writing. "But let's be realistic. I haven't written even one column yet."

"You'll be my only famous friend." Deborah was like a terrier digging for a bone. She wouldn't abandon the subject.

"Your sister isn't so excited." Eleanor noticed that, though she'd been the one who'd started the discussion of fame, Virginia's face had turned sober.

"It's a wonderful opportunity for you, but . . ." Her voice trailed off, her expression transmitting her discomfort. "Maybe I'm being a worrywart, but I'm concerned about you working late at night."

Eleanor tugged off her second boot and placed it on the floor next to its mate. "All I have to do is write the column. Brad will do the rest."

Though she'd been perfectly serious, something about Eleanor's response made Virginia smile. "That may be all you *have* to do," her friend said, "but is it all you will do? I know you, Eleanor. You'll want to oversee every aspect of getting your column published. Won't you?"

"Well . . . maybe." Virginia's argument was difficult to refute. Eleanor suspected she'd be as anxious as Brad was the day before the first edition of the *Herald* was published. "Maybe."

"Definitely." Deborah wrinkled her nose. "Definitely before the Hudson flows upstream."

All three of them laughed at the quip. "You're both right," Eleanor agreed. "I'll want to be there to see the type set and to read the first copy off the presses. At least the first few times."

"That's what I'm worried about," Virginia said. "You'll be walking home alone after dark. Hidden Falls is very safe during the day, but you never know who might be out at night."

"Brad will be with me." Eleanor knew without asking that he'd insist on accompanying her back to her boardinghouse.

"What if he's not? What if there's something that keeps him at the paper? Could you protect yourself?"

"I can run."

Deborah shook her head. "Men have the advantage. They have longer legs and no skirts to hamper them. That means they can run faster. Virginia's right. You need to know how to fight."

"Fight?" Pugilism was one subject Eleanor's finishing school had not included in its curriculum.

"Fight. Defend yourself." Virginia's expression remained serious. "It's important."

"We have two older brothers," Deborah explained. "We learned a lot from them."

Virginia nodded. "We'll teach you, starting tomorrow evening."

"You want to start an evening school as well as a lyceum?" Brad gave Eleanor a long appraising look. They were sitting on the steps outside the newspaper office, reviewing the plans for the lyceum. As promised, he'd started making arrangements. "Before you're done, you'll have transformed Moreland Mills' workers' lives."

Brad was wrong. Though she hoped there would indeed be a transformation, she wouldn't be the person responsible for it. "They're the ones who'll make the changes. All we're doing is giving them an opportunity." Though Brad appeared sympathetic, Eleanor wanted to be certain he understood what was at stake. "They're so eager to learn and improve themselves." Most of the mill workers were farmers' daughters who had completed the eighth grade but wanted more. It amazed Eleanor that, as tired as they were at the end of the work day, they still sought opportunities to improve themselves, borrowing books from the lending library and attending every cultural event the town offered.

"I think of what we're doing as providing a meal. The lyceum lectures are desserts. They taste delicious, but the girls need more."

"And the evening classes you're proposing are the meat, potatoes, and vegetables?" As if he knew it would amuse her, Brad pretended to cut and eat a piece of food.

"Exactly."

"This tastes good," he said with a mischievous grin. "What flavors . . . er, what subjects did you think we should offer?"

Not the ones Virginia and Deborah had taught her. Over the course of several evenings, Eleanor had learned to step on the arch of a man's foot, to punch his nose, and to jab his eyes. Though she didn't deny the potential value of those classes, the art of foiling an attacker wasn't a subject the other mill hands craved. They sought a more classical education.

Eleanor held up her hand and began turning down fingers as she said, "History, geometry, composition, maybe French or German, and music lessons—voice and piano. That's to start. We can add more next year." *But I won't be here.* She swallowed, trying to dissolve the lump that had settled in her throat. She'd known from the beginning that her stay in Hidden Falls would be temporary. In a year she'd be free of Uncle Abel and his threats. She could return to New York and establish a life there. Why did that prospect suddenly seem unappealing?

"That's a rather comprehensive list." Brad's voice was neutral, giving no hint of his feelings.

"Do you agree with the concept?" That was the critical question. Without Brad's support, Eleanor had little chance of turning her dream into reality. Though he was estranged from his parents, he still bore the Harrod name and the power it conferred.

"I like it," he said. "And for more than one reason. Besides being a good idea for Hidden Falls, it might help a friend of mine." Brad looked into the distance for a moment, his expression pensive. "Did I ever tell you about Anthony?" he asked as he turned back toward Eleanor. "In college, he, Charles, and I were nicknamed the ABCs, not just because of our names but also because we were inseparable. Next to Charles, Anthony is my best friend."

Eleanor recalled Charles alluding to Anthony and some kind of pact the three men had had. "Is Anthony still in Boston?"

Brad shook his head. "He married and has been traveling in Europe." Before Eleanor could respond, Brad added, "His wife died."

What could anyone say that wouldn't sound trite? "How sad!"

Brad nodded, his voice slightly husky as he explained, "I want to help him build a new life, and this might be a good opportunity." Eleanor's expression must have been quizzical, for Brad said, "I forgot to mention a critical factor. Anthony is a professor. A very good one."

No wonder Brad thought the evening classes would benefit his friend. "Perfect."

"I'll write Anthony a letter tonight." Brad's expression was once again cheerful. "Now, let me tell you what I've arranged for the lyceum."

Wishing she weren't in the first row, Eleanor turned as discreetly as she could. She hadn't been mistaken. The church was filled. There were even people standing in the back. Wonderful! Brad had said he'd had no problem convincing the church elders to allow them to use the building for the lyceum lectures. After all, Hidden Falls had a long history of conducting town meetings and other public gatherings, including the quarterly musicales, in the beautiful white building with the wedding-cake steeple. The lectures would be another in the list of illustrious civic events.

Eleanor had been pleased when she'd heard the decision. Now she was more than pleased, for tonight there was not a spare seat. It appeared that not only had all the mill workers come to the inaugural lecture, but so too had most of the townspeople. Unlike the last musicale, which many of the permanent residents had boycotted because it had included Deborah's duet with another mill hand, no one was shunning tonight's entertainment.

"I haven't seen the church this crowded since Easter," Susannah Moreland murmured.

Eleanor smiled. Though she'd protested when Brad had insisted she sit in front with Charles and Susannah and Charles's sister Anne, he had been adamant. "I'll be there for most of the evening," he had pointed out. "Besides, this was your idea. You ought to share in the glory."

Eleanor hadn't wanted glory—at least not for herself. What she wanted was a successful beginning to the lyceum. She'd agreed to the seating arrangement only when Brad agreed not to introduce her or to mention her role in establishing the lecture series.

"This was a great idea." Susannah's words brought Eleanor back to the present. "A great idea for everyone except Rob. I've never seen him so nervous, except maybe on the day we first opened the carousel." Susannah turned to the woman on her other side, Rob's wife, Anne. "That evening Rob was worried you wouldn't like it."

Though Eleanor couldn't imagine anyone not being enchanted by Rob Ludlow's masterpiece, she understood his stakes had been higher than most people realized. For

Rob the merry-go-round had been more than twenty-four animals. It had been his first gift to the woman he loved.

No matter how often she heard the story, Eleanor's heart never failed to be touched, and she'd find herself wiping away tears of joy. The three Moreland siblings' romances were the stuff of legend in Hidden Falls, a reminder that true love existed and that dreams could come true. The mill workers recounted the tales of star-crossed lovers who somehow managed to find their happily-ever-after in the same hushed tones Eleanor's mother once used when reciting fairytales.

As the bedtime stories had so many years ago, the Moreland romances filled Eleanor with longing. Perhaps someday she would have a love story of her own, the story of a man who loved her enough to surmount seemingly impossible obstacles, the story of a man she loved so much that she'd risk everything—even her life—for him. It was a wonderful dream, and maybe—just maybe—it would come true someday.

"Ladies and gentlemen." For tonight's presentation they had moved a podium to the center front. Brad stood beside it, waiting until the crowd's murmuring ceased before he continued. "I'm not going to waste your time by telling you what a landmark event this is. If you've read the *Herald,* you already know that." A ripple of laughter greeted his self-promotion. "Instead, let's get to the important part of the evening. It is my pleasure to introduce a man of undeniable talent, a man whose work has received acclaim across the country, a man who could live anywhere but who's now made Hidden Falls his home. Please join me in welcoming the lyceum lecture series' first speaker: Rob Ludlow."

As the applause subsided, Rob took his place at the podium, and Brad slid into the pew next to Eleanor. "So far, so good," he murmured. Eleanor smiled, as much at the fact that Brad was sitting close enough that she could feel the warmth radiating from his arm as at the reception his introduction had received. She settled back in the pew and focused her attention on the speaker.

Rob gave the audience a wry grin. "I suppose I ought to thank Brad, but that's a mighty fancy way to describe a simple woodcarver." As he had probably intended, the audience laughed. What Rob did was anything but simple carving. "It gives me more pleasure than I can express to know that you ride and enjoy the painted ponies I create," he continued. "Tonight I'm going to try to show you how it's done."

For the next hour, the audience was virtually mesmerized by Rob's description of the process and his explanation of the lingo carvers used. He'd brought examples with him, showing how he started with a preliminary sketch of the animal, then glued blocks of wood together to form what he called a "blank." The challenge, he explained, was to first "boast" and then "release" the animal from that block of wood, using gouges and chisels. Boasting, Rob said with a grin, was the carving of the rough shape, while releasing created the fine details. Only when both were finished and the animal had been carefully sanded could he and his assistants begin the work of painting, a process that involved four coats of primer before the colored paint and the gems and gold leaf that turned the animals from ordinary into magnificent could be applied.

As he spoke, the church was silent, the townspeople obviously rapt in their attention to everything Rob was saying and showing. It was a wonderful presentation, and yet Eleanor found her mind wandering. When Rob spoke of boasting, she darted a glance at Brad, wondering whether he would ever boast of his success with the paper. The almost imperceptible shake of his head coupled with the crooked smile told her he'd somehow understood her unspoken question, and that brought an unexpected flush to Eleanor's cheeks.

How embarrassing it would be if he was truly able to read her mind! For if he could, he'd realize that she was not immune to his presence, that her pulse had accelerated when he'd taken the seat next to her, that her heart thudded when his hand had brushed hers, and that she wished with all her heart she'd been able to give him a different answer when he'd requested permission to court her.

Her life had become complex, thanks to the web of half-truths she'd spun. Brad, like everyone else in Hidden Falls, believed Eleanor came from a humble background. What would happen if they all learned the truth? It was possible she'd lose her position at the mill, for Moreland Mills had high standards. Lack of honesty, no matter the reason, was a serious offense. Even if she kept her job, how would the other mill hands react? Would they distance themselves from her? The prospect was painful, as was the possibility that her fledgling plans for the lyceum and evening classes might be abandoned. Eleanor couldn't let that happen.

Then there was Brad. Though she knew he'd deny it, Eleanor couldn't ignore the fear that part of his attraction to her was based on her being a mill worker. She knew he'd been hurt by Jane Moreland's rejection. What better way to show his indifference to that slight than by courting a woman on the opposite end of the social spectrum? Brad's rift with his parents was equally well known. Was his desire to court her an act of rebellion against his parents?

Further complicating her life were Uncle Abel and his threats. He would, of course, have no power over her if she were to marry Brad, but Eleanor couldn't do that. As she'd told Brad, she wasn't ready for marriage, and she didn't believe he was either. Perhaps someday . . .

Thunderous applause marked the end of Rob's speech and brought Eleanor back to the present. She smiled at the man behind the podium, hoping he hadn't realized how far her thoughts had wandered. When Rob had responded to the audience's questions, he nodded toward Brad, who rose and joined him.

"Thank you, ladies and gentlemen." Brad smiled at the assembly. "I hope you'll agree with me that no one can match our first speaker's eloquence. I won't even try." A low murmur greeted his words. "Yes, I'm scheduled to deliver our next lecture. That will be three weeks from today. In the meantime, though, I have a surprise for you. The carousel is now open for rides."

To Eleanor's amusement, the normally staid towns-people practically tripped over each other in their rush to the door.

"Oh, Brad, this was wonderful," she told him half an hour later as they dimmed the lights and closed the door behind them. Though Charles and Susannah had offered to help with the cleanup, Brad had insisted they join Rob and Anne as hosts at the merry-go-round. He and Eleanor, he announced, needed no assistance, a claim that caused Susannah to raise her eyebrows and hurry her husband out the door.

"You picked the perfect person for our first lecture," Eleanor continued.

Brad shrugged as if the decision had been trivial. "We said our goal was to help promote pride in Hidden Falls. What better way than to feature our own citizens? Although," he admitted, "I'm not so sure about being next on the list. Producing a newspaper isn't as glamorous as carving ponies."

"You must not have been listening to Rob." Eleanor wondered if Brad's attention had wandered as much as hers had. Nonsense. Just because he'd shared dozens of private smiles with her didn't mean he wasn't focused on his friend's presentation. "Everything Rob said pointed to the fact that building a carousel is a lot of hard work. All the fun comes once the horses are done. You know, Brad, that sounds a lot like publishing the *Herald.* In fact, it's probably the same as many jobs.

The pleasure comes at the end." Eleanor grinned. "That's one of the reasons this was a great beginning for the lyceum. Rob talked about something unique, but we could all share his feelings. I can't imagine anything more perfect."

They had crossed Bridge Street and were walking slowly toward the park. Even from this distance, the sound of the Würlitzer organ filled the air, luring people to the carousel. As a small group of people who'd been strolling ahead of increased their pace, Brad slowed his steps, stopping under one of the large oak trees that lined this part of Bridge. Deliberately, as if he had all the time in the world, he removed Eleanor's hand from his arm and turned to face her. This time his action filled her not with regret but with anticipation, for the look he gave her was warm and tender. He smiled slowly, the faint moonlight revealing an expression she'd never before seen.

"I can imagine something more perfect," Brad said, his voice low and husky. Slowly, he drew her into his arms. For a long moment, he gazed down at her, his eyes seeming to ask a question at the same time they shone with an emotion so powerful she hesitated to name it. She must have nodded or given him some sign, for Brad's mouth softened into a smile before he lowered his lips to hers.

Though Eleanor had thought about it and dreamed about it, thoughts and dreams paled against the reality of their first embrace. Brad's kiss was warm and tender, the gentle touch of his lips on hers sending shivers of delight through her veins. As he drew her ever closer, his arms enfolding her in his embrace, Eleanor knew that he was right. This was perfection, pure and simple, the perfect ending to a perfect day.

"I'm getting mighty tired of your excuses, Abel." It wasn't the first time Clifford Warren had appeared at his home, demanding to know when Abel would produce Eleanor, but tonight was different. Tonight it appeared Clifford had imbibed more than a little whiskey, for his words were slurred, his expression more belligerent than usual.

"What kind of man can't figure out where his niece has gone to?" Abel's unwelcome visitor continued the interrogation. "She's only a girl. How far can she have gone?"

"We'll find her soon." Though Abel felt a rivulet of sweat make the way down the back of his neck, he hoped his voice did not betray his discomfort. Clifford must not guess that it wasn't the summer heat that made Abel perspire but his continued failure to find the missing heiress. "Soon," he repeated. It was essential to placate Clifford, even if it involved telling a few lies. The man was key to his plans. If Clifford decided to find a different wife, it would take Abel months—perhaps even longer—to find another man desperate enough to marry his wayward niece. "This is a big city, you know. That's why it's taking so long to find her. She could be anywhere. But it won't be long now. She'll run out of money soon."

Clifford's face reddened with barely suppressed

anger. "That's what you said last month. I thought you took away her allowance."

"I did, and she hasn't gotten any money from her banker. I know that for a fact." The conversation with the man who served as trustee for Eleanor's inheritance had been one of the more unpleasant hours Abel had had to endure since he'd taken charge of that thankless girl.

The banker hadn't smiled once. Oh, no, not even when Abel had recounted one of his favorite jokes. Instead, that stone-faced man had announced that he had received a letter from Eleanor, stating that since she was no longer living in her uncle's home, Abel should have no further access to her money. The banker had been adamant, pointing out that the only reason Abel had been receiving those monthly checks—generous checks, the man had said—was that the money was to have been used for Eleanor's welfare. No Eleanor, no checks.

The banker wouldn't listen to reason. Abel had used every bit of persuasion he could muster, all to no avail. The stone-faced man wasn't going to part with a penny. And, to make it worse, Abel's personal attorney had confirmed the banker's decision. No one seemed to care that Abel had debts to be paid and men who were becoming increasingly insistent that those debts be paid immediately.

"So, what are you gonna do?" Clifford demanded.

He was going to find that worthless, ungrateful wretch, that's what he was going to do. And when he found her . . . Abel had spent days planning exactly what he was going to do to Miss Interfering Eleanor Menger when he had her in his clutches. But those were things he had no intention of sharing with the man who had agreed to marry her and share her fortune with Abel.

"I've already done it," he said, infusing his voice with pride. "I hired an investigator." And that man had better find her quickly, or Abel wasn't sure how he would pay him either.

"A Pinkerton?" For the first time, Clifford appeared pleased.

"Just as good." But less expensive. Much less expensive. "Mark my words, Clifford. Eleanor will be your wife within a month." She had to be.

Chapter Eight

"**I** wish you'd signed your name." Millie waved the newspaper in front of Eleanor as they walked the last few yards to the mill.

Eleanor shrugged, not wanting to explain that Brad had also encouraged her to admit authorship, and she'd refused, claiming she was nothing more than a spokesperson for the other workers and was loath to take credit when they were the ones who deserved the accolades.

That was part of the truth. The other part was that, though she told herself it was irrational, she feared signing her name might somehow lead Uncle Abel to Hidden Falls. For what seemed like the millionth time, Eleanor wished she'd had the forethought to use a pseudonym when she'd left New York. She'd donned someone else's clothes; why hadn't she thought to assume a false name? But she hadn't, and so she'd let Brad print only her initials.

"I loved the way you used your Hudson River phrase," Deborah said. The paper had been delivered to the boardinghouse before dinner and, though normally Mrs. Weld had a strict policy about not reading anything at the table, she'd relaxed her rules today and had, in fact, read Eleanor's column aloud so everyone could enjoy it. To Eleanor's delight, her fellow boarders had laughed at the correct times and had seemed genuinely pleased by her portrayal of their role in Hidden Falls.

Virginia nodded, apparently agreeing with her sister. "Are you going to use that phrase in every column? It could become your signature line."

"I hadn't thought about it," Eleanor admitted. The truth was, her reference to the river had been nothing more than an attempt to add some levity. Like Brad, she believed in the value of humor, particularly when dealing with a subject as serious—and as important—as the mill workers. When she'd used her euphemism for *never,* she'd been worried about the way her words might be received. Would the mill hands be pleased by the portrait she'd painted? Would the townspeople scoff when they read about a mill worker's daily life, or would they appreciate the effort and undeniable skill that went into producing the textiles they used?

Though Brad had told her she had no cause to fret, Eleanor had not believed him. Brad, after all, was not an impartial judge. He was her friend and—oh, why deny it?—he was more than that. The kiss they'd shared had changed everything. It had lasted only a few seconds, certainly less than a minute, and yet when it ended, Eleanor had realized she could never again regard Brad as simply a friend. The feelings he'd stirred in her were deeper, stronger, more wonderful than anything she'd experienced. In that moment, her mind accepted what her heart had known all along, that Brad was special and that, if this were a perfect world, she would have given him another answer when he'd asked to court her.

"You should."

Eleanor blinked as she heard Deborah's words. What was it she ought to do? Tell Brad he could woo her? No! Deborah was talking about the column she had written and what Deborah called Eleanor's signature line. That was all. Eleanor took a deep breath as she thanked the stars Deborah hadn't been able to read her mind. The two sisters had been more than a little intrigued by her friendship with Brad and had made no secret of the fact that they hoped it would turn into something more serious. Eleanor had dismissed the suggestion each time it was raised, insisting she and Brad were friends and business associates—surely the work she was doing for the *Herald* qualified them for that distinction—but nothing more.

She shook her head, trying to clear it. They were almost at the mill, and here she was, still thinking about Brad. Once inside, she would need to concentrate on her looms. Just this week, Mr. Greeley had assigned her a second loom. That was good, of course. Not only did it double her pay, but it also meant that Eleanor was no longer an apprentice, since she'd been judged capable of handling a full workload. The problem was, running two looms seemed to demand five times as much attention as one had. Though Virginia assured her she'd soon become accustomed to the increased pace, Eleanor knew it would take weeks, if not months to acquire that level of skill. In the meantime, she had to be careful, lest she injure herself on the fast-moving equipment.

When she entered the weaving room, Eleanor heard a round of cheers and applause. She paused, startled by the unexpected noise. "It's for you," Deborah said. "They're proud of you."

"You made us look important," one of the women told Eleanor.

"We are important." That was one of the things Eleanor hoped readers would understand from her column. "Hardly anyone in Hidden Falls would have a job if it weren't for us."

The woman shrugged. "I don't reckon anybody thought of that 'til you pointed it out. Thanks, Eleanor."

"You said things I been thinkin'," a second woman added, "but I didn't know the right words."

"I sure wish I could write like you." It was Millie who chimed in, her voice wistful. "Words just run away when I pick up a pen."

Eleanor couldn't help smiling at the image of runaway words. "But you're much more skilled at the loom than I'll ever be." It wasn't idle flattery. Millie was widely acknowledged to be the best weaver.

"That's nothing." Her voice left no doubt that Millie believed her words.

Eleanor shook a finger at her, pretending to admonish her. "I thought you read my column," she said with feigned seriousness. "If you had, you'd know that weaving is *not* nothing."

"She's right, Millie." The second woman nodded her head. "What we do is important."

The glow of pleasure that swept through Eleanor did not subside, not even when the bobbin on her second loom became stuck and it took Eleanor precious minutes to dislodge it. As annoying as that was, nothing could diminish her sense of satisfaction. Almost from the first day, she had wanted these women to understand the role they played in Hidden Falls and to be proud of it. If what she heard was true—and she had no reason to doubt it—her column had helped them take the first step on that journey.

"I have good news." Though he should have been working on the next issue of the paper, Brad couldn't wait to share his news with Charles.

The owner of Moreland Mills perched on the edge of the desk, a grin on his face. At the moment he looked more like the instigator of far too many childhood pranks than a successful businessman. "Let me guess. Your Eleanor has agreed to marry you?"

His Eleanor? Marriage? Brad was flummoxed. "What makes you say that?" Just because he spent an inordinate amount of time dreaming about marrying Eleanor didn't mean he'd told Charles about it. No, indeed. Brad had been careful not to discuss weddings or anything even remotely connected to them.

"Why would I think you want to marry Eleanor? No reason," Charles said slowly, "except . . ." He paused for emphasis. "How about the fact that every time you're with her, you look happier than I've ever seen you? Or when she's in the room, even if you're talking to someone else—like me—you keep looking at her? And when she's not around, every other sentence has her name in it. Or . . ."

Brad had had enough. "That's not true." Surely it wasn't. "You're exaggerating." He'd been careful, so very careful not to reveal his feelings. It appeared he had not been careful enough.

"It is true." Charles slid off his desk and stood next to Brad. "You're in love, my friend, and I couldn't be happier for you."

Though this conversation was not what he had expected, perhaps there was one thing to be gained. Perhaps Brad could ask a question that had been plaguing him. "Do you mean that if I were to ask Eleanor to marry me—which, I must point out, I have not done—and if she were to accept me—which I'm not at all certain she would—if that happened, would you and Susannah approve?"

Tiny furrows appeared between Charles's eyes. "What made you think we would object? Surely it's not the fact that she works at the mill."

That was the very reason Brad had expected resistance. "You weren't exactly in favor of your sister marrying a mill worker's son, even though he had a fancy degree from Harvard." Eleanor had no such distinction. All she had was dignity, decency, and a desire to help others.

A frown crossed Charles's face. Turning abruptly, as if reluctant to reveal his feelings, he grabbed his cup and headed toward the small table where a pot of coffee could always be found. "You're right that I didn't think Matt was good enough for Jane, but it had nothing to do with Matt's family. It was Matt himself."

Though Brad and Charles had shared many secrets, Matt Wagner had always been off limits. "You never did like him, did you?"

"Not when we were growing up," Charles admitted, "but we've settled our differences. He makes Jane happy, and that's what's important."

Charles was polite enough not to state the obvious: marriage to Brad would not have brought his sister happiness. It was amazing, Brad realized, how things worked out for the best. At the time, Jane's refusal to marry him had been a disappointment. Now he knew how fortunate they both were that she'd had the good sense to refuse him.

"Speaking hypothetically of course, how do you think the townspeople would react if I did marry Eleanor?" Brad addressed the words to his friend's back.

Charles reached for the coffee pot and poured himself another cup, as if he needed an infusion of caffeine to answer the question. "I'm not sure." His words confirmed

Brad's fears. "A year ago, I would have said the reaction would have been unfavorable, but that was before Jane married Matt and before your Eleanor started her campaign to bring the town and the mill closer."

His Eleanor. That was twice Charles had referred to her that way. Though Brad had never used the term, he liked the way it sounded on Charles's lips.

"She's an eloquent advocate," Charles continued. He was once more seated on the edge of his desk, the cup of coffee next to him.

"She's that and so much more."

"And you're cap over boots in love with her."

There was no point in denying it. As his best friend, Charles had always been able to read Brad's moods. "I'm also more scared than I've ever been that she'll refuse me."

"Why would she do that, other than that you're an ugly, ornery critter?"

This was the Charles he'd always known, the one who'd cloak his feelings in sarcasm. "Thanks, old man." It was a term that Charles hated, the traditional response to being called ugly and ornery. For a moment, Brad was transported back a dozen years to a time when he and Charles had traded secrets and solemn vows in the cave they'd dug by the river's edge. "I appreciate your high regard."

"Seriously, Brad, it's your parents' reaction you ought to be worrying about, not Eleanor's. She'd be a fool to refuse you, and I have to say that she never struck me as a fool."

"I hope you're right."

"I'm always right. Just ask Susannah." Charles drained the coffee. "Now, what was your good news?"

Brad had almost forgotten the reason he'd come to Charles's office. He patted the envelope that he'd stuffed in his pocket. "Anthony agreed to come to Hidden Falls. He'll be in charge of both the lyceum and the evening school."

Charles grinned. "You're right. That is good news. It'll be like old times with the ABCs together again. Come to think of it, it'll be better than old times. We'll all be together for your wedding. What could be better?"

Assuming there was a wedding, Brad could think of nothing better.

"It's a pleasant evening. I wondered if I could convince you to walk with me."

Eleanor tried not to stare at Brad. While his words were ordinary, he seemed oddly ill at ease as he stood by the front door of her boardinghouse. Try though she might, Eleanor could not find a reason for his nervousness. The paper had been put to bed, meaning that it was ready to print, so she doubted he was worried about the next issue, and they'd already celebrated the accolades the previous issues had received. But if the *Herald* wasn't the cause for the nervous tremor in Brad's voice, what was? The only cause Eleanor could imagine was another falling-out with his parents.

The townspeople continued to speculate on how long the estrangement would last, noting that Mrs. Harrod had been seen on Main Street less frequently than normal and that Brad's father was spending more days in New York than previously. Both parents, the grapevine claimed, were avoiding possible encounters with their son. Perhaps something else had occurred between them and Brad needed a friend to cheer him. If so, she'd be that friend.

"I'd enjoy a stroll," Eleanor said truthfully. She'd been working on her next column for the *Herald* and had reached a deadlock. Two ideas were competing for importance, with the result that she'd been unable to form a coherent sentence. Some time away might clear her mind.

A few minutes later, Eleanor returned, wearing her hat and gloves, ready for a trip downtown. Though the carousel was not running tonight, she imagined they'd walk toward their normal destination, the park. Instead Brad turned left when they reached Mill Street.

"Am I permitted to ask our destination?" As far as Eleanor knew, there was nothing to see on this part of Mill. The road dead-ended a hundred or so yards past the mill complex. Beyond that a dense forest extended from the river's edge to the northern town limits.

"I suspect you've not seen our falls." She must have imagined Brad's earlier nervousness, for now his voice sounded normal.

"That's true." Eleanor chuckled. "The town is well named, since the falls really are hidden." Although the mill harnessed power from the cataract to run its equipment, a bend in the river kept the falls invisible from the mill itself. "Virginia and Deborah have promised to take me to the overlook, but we've been either too busy or too tired to make the trip." They'd told her it would require close to an hour each way.

When they reached the end of the road, Brad turned right, leading Eleanor into the midst of the thicket. "I feel as if that's my fault. I should have realized writing for the *Herald* would only make you busier and more tired," he said as he held a branch so she could walk beneath it. "I'm sorry."

"Don't be sorry. I enjoy writing." It was the mill work that caused her fatigue, not the *Herald*. That was invigorating, except for days like today when she encountered barriers. "I feel as if you've opened doors for me and that writing could be my future after I leave the mill."

Those doors were figurative. Right now Brad was opening more literal ones, pushing bushes and vine tendrils aside so Eleanor could walk. Though they were only a few yards off the road, the underbrush was so thick that she could no longer see Mill Street. As for the path they followed, while Brad appeared to have no trouble finding it, to Eleanor it appeared narrow and overgrown. If this was the way to the falls, it was an unpopular route.

Brad didn't seem to mind or even to notice. Though he walked next to her, clearing the path, he appeared deep in thought. "That's what I'd like to talk to you about," he said. "Your future."

Once again, Brad's voice was uncharacteristically

serious, reminding her of the nervousness she'd noticed when he'd come to the boardinghouse. Wanting to lighten his mood, Eleanor shook her head. "It's much too beautiful a day to worry about the future. What I want to know is why we're going this direction. I understood the only place to see the falls was on the opposite side of the river." Deborah had described crossing the river and walking past the three huge houses on the hill before reaching a path that descended to the falls overlook.

"That's what most people think. They're mistaken." Brad took a step forward, then turned, extending his hand to guide Eleanor over a fallen log. "Careful of your skirts." Though Eleanor had thought it impossible, the path narrowed again, becoming little more than a rabbit trail. Vegetation was quickly obliterating any trace of human passage, while long tendrils of vines extending from the bushes made walking perilous. "I'm sorry," Brad repeated. "We should probably turn around. This is more overgrown than I remembered."

He was right. They should not be here. It was wild and unruly, not a place a lady would choose for a stroll. She and Brad were defying a major social convention, being here alone. Still, Eleanor didn't care. "It's beautiful." She reached for a branch. "Look at this, Brad. They're wild raspberries." Though the fruit was not yet ripe, the berries were obviously thriving, perhaps because the sharp thorns discouraged birds and small animals from coming too close. "This is the first time I've seen a raspberry vine."

Brad laughed, his good humor seemingly restored. "Now you can't claim there are no advantages to living here."

"I never said there weren't." The truth was, though she'd been surprised by it, Eleanor had found she did not miss her former life and had no desire to return to the city.

"Then you like living in Hidden Falls?" Was that relief she heard in his voice?

Eleanor nodded. "Much more than I expected." When she'd come to Hidden Falls, she'd viewed the town as a sanctuary, a place to spend eleven months. She had not expected to find friends there or to have the town become her home. But both had happened.

They'd been walking slowly, picking their way through the brush. Now Brad stopped and faced her. "I know you came for the same reason as the other mill workers, to earn money." That was true, even if it was only part of what had brought Eleanor to the small town. She nodded.

Brad's eyes deepened to emerald, a sign of the intensity of his feelings. "I was hoping you'd consider staying in Hidden Falls permanently."

Once again, Eleanor tried to defuse the tension that was so strong she could feel it in the grip of his hand. "I understand. You want me to continue writing a column for the *Herald*."

Though she'd expected him to laugh, he did not. "That would be a bonus, but . . ."

"Are those the falls I hear?" Perhaps it was rude to

interrupt Brad, but Eleanor's instincts told her not to continue this conversation. The gleam in his eyes reminded her of his expression on Independence Day when he'd asked permission to court her. No matter how wonderful their kiss had been, no matter how deeply she cared for him, Eleanor was not ready to speak of love and marriage. She tugged on Brad's hand. "I want to see the water."

In less than a minute, they had reached the end of the trail and stood on the riverbank. "Oh, Brad, it's beautiful!" It was also far different from what she had expected. The Sempert sisters had described the overlook on the other side of the river. Based on their description, Eleanor had expected to be at eye level with the falls themselves. She was not. Brad's trail had led them to the base. From here, Eleanor could see the cataract tumbling over the edge, swirling over boulders at the bottom, sending up plumes of mist that refracted the light into tiny rainbows.

"This is magnificent." She'd seen pictures of Niagara and Yosemite. As beautiful as they were, surely nothing could compare to this, the natural wonder that defined her new home and gave work to so many.

Brad seemed pleased by her reaction. "Dare I hope that's another reason for you to remain here?"

He wasn't going to abandon the subject, no matter how much she tried to redirect it. "I don't understand," she said, keeping her voice light. "You're acting as if I'm ready to leave. I assure you, my departure is not imminent."

Brad wrinkled his nose. "I'm making a mash of it again. I know you told me I need to wait, but I can't." His words tumbled out with the force of the waterfalls. "I love you, Eleanor. I want to marry you. Please say you'll be my wife."

For a second Eleanor was silent. This was what she had feared. Marriage was a wonderful dream, but it was one that could not come true, not now, perhaps not ever. He had to know that. She'd tried to avoid the whole subject, since it could only cause pain. Now there was no alternative. She would have to hurt this dear man again. "Oh, Brad, I can't."

His eyes darkened, and the tightening of his lips told her he had not expected her refusal. Why would he, when they'd shared that wonderful kiss? Eleanor closed her eyes for a second, remembering just how marvelous that moment had been. Perhaps she should regret it, but she couldn't, for Brad's kiss had been the sweetest moment of her life.

Furrows formed between Brad's eyes. "If you think I care that you work in the mill, I don't, and neither do my friends. You won't be shunned by the townspeople, if that's what you fear."

That was not the source of Eleanor's fears. Though she might not like it, she knew she could endure a shunning. "You might be," she countered. She would address this concern before she pointed out the significant omission in Brad's declaration. Though he'd said he and his friends were not bothered by her social status, there had been no mention of his parents. Without asking, Eleanor knew the older Harrods would not approve of her as a daughter-in-law.

"I heard it was Jane who suffered the most when she was first engaged to Matt Wagner."

Brad shook his head as if dismissing her concerns. "I doubt that will happen, but I don't care if it does. I love you, Eleanor. You're more important than anything in my life. Without you, my days are gray and empty."

Those were the words she'd longed to her, the ones she'd let herself dream he would one day pronounce. They should fill her heart with gladness. Instead, Eleanor felt only regret that their love could not follow the normal path and lead to marriage.

"Oh, Brad, I wish . . ." She let the words trail off as he took her right hand, clasping it between both of his.

"My father once accused me of not knowing what I wanted in life." Brad's lips quirked in a wry smile. "Though I didn't agree, he may have been right at the time. But that's not true anymore. I know what I want." Brad tightened the grip on her hand. "I want you—as my wife, my helpmate, and the mother of my children."

What could she say? She wanted all of those things too. The difference was, she knew how great a price Brad would have to pay for them. As Eleanor tried to phrase her reply, he continued, "I know you may not love me as much as I love you, but if you love me even a little, that will be enough."

Though she couldn't make his dream—and hers— come true, Eleanor couldn't let him believe he was unloved. "I do love you, Brad." She gave his hand a little squeeze. "I tried to fight my feelings, but I lost."

For the first time since they'd reached the river, Brad grinned. "I'm glad. Your loss means I've won. Say you'll marry me."

They had come full circle. "I can't."

"You're not making sense. If you love me—and you just said you did—why can't you marry me?"

"Because of your parents." When he started to interrupt, Eleanor shook her head. "Let me finish. I know you're estranged from them, and that disturbs me deeply." It wasn't that the townspeople were vocal in their disapproval. Like Brad, Eleanor knew they could weather gossip, innuendos, and even outright hostility. What concerned her was the effect of the rift on both Brad and his parents.

"I was blessed with loving parents." She smiled as she pictured the three of them together. Life hadn't always been happy, but it had been filled with love. She couldn't let Brad forfeit that.

Eleanor looked at the man she loved so dearly and said, "Even though they were taken from me far too early, I treasure the memories of our years together. I think of Mama and Papa's love as the golden thread that makes the fabric of my life special." Brad was listening. What wasn't clear was whether he understood the importance of family.

"I don't know the reason for the rift between you and your parents, but I can't believe that marrying me would help it. I suspect it would only make it worse."

The tightening of Brad's lips confirmed Eleanor's supposition. "It doesn't matter."

"Yes, it does—to me and to you. Can you honestly say that they'd approve of our marriage?"

He hesitated before he said, "They would if they knew you."

It was as she had feared. "But they don't know me, and they probably never will." There was no reason for their paths to cross.

Suddenly Brad's face brightened. "That's the answer, then. My parents need to get to know you."

"Brad, I didn't expect you." A smile wreathed his mother's face. "Does this mean you've decided to come home?"

"It's something different." He wouldn't say "no," although that was the truth. If Eleanor accepted his proposal, this would never again be his home. Even if she did not—and that was a prospect he did not want to consider—Brad doubted he'd ever feel comfortable returning to his childhood home. "Perhaps we could go into the parlor." Surely being in his mother's favorite room would help her consider his request more favorably.

When they were seated and Brad had declined the offer of refreshment, he took a deep breath. Giving his mother his warmest smile, he said, "I wanted to tell you that I've asked Eleanor to marry me."

Any hope he had of maternal approval was destroyed by the shocked look on his mother's face. "That girl?

The mill hand?" Her normally well-modulated voice was little less than a screech.

This was not going the way he had hoped. Brad tried another tactic. "Eleanor is the beautiful, intelligent, caring woman I want to share my life. And, yes, Mother, she does happen to work at the mill."

His mother gripped the chair arms as if they were a lifeline. "Have you taken leave of your senses?" she demanded. "What can you possibly see in her?" Without waiting for an answer, she added, "I don't have to ask what the girl sees in you. She thinks you're her chance to escape the mill." Mother took a deep breath, exhaling slowly in the way Brad had seen her do so often before when she was trying to control her anger. This was one of the few times that anger had been directed at Brad. "Have you told her you won't have an inheritance?" Now she sounded like Father. He was the one who favored pecuniary threats.

"As strange as it may seem, Mother, Eleanor does not care about my money. She cares about me and about you."

"Me?" His mother's carefully groomed eyebrows rose an inch, and she laced her voice laced with scorn as she continued, "The chit doesn't know me. She's a scheming wretch who'll say anything to get your ring on her finger."

Brad clenched his fists, trying to control his anger. He'd inherited his mother's hasty temper as well as her red hair. "Careful, Mother. That's my future wife you're talking about." It took every ounce of self-control he possessed to keep his voice even. "For the record, Eleanor is not like that. She's not scheming. She is not a chit or a wretch, and I'd appreciate it if you'd refer to her by her name."

"Be that as it may, she's all wrong for you." Mother was in one of her stubborn moods, refusing to pronounce Eleanor's name. "How will you ever take her out in polite company? Why, she probably eats peas off her knife."

"I think you'd be surprised. Eleanor may work at the mill, but she's a lady."

"Preposterous!"

It was the opportunity Brad had sought. As casually as if the thought had just occurred to him, he said, "Shall we see who's right? I'll bring Eleanor here for dinner, and you can observe her manners. Just think, Mother, that will give you a chance to see what kind of person she is. All I ask is that you and Father agree to be civil to her."

There was a long silence as his mother considered the proposition. Brad saw the gleam in her eyes, and the calculating expression told him she was confident Eleanor would embarrass not only herself but Brad. "What do I get in return?" she asked in a surprisingly cordial voice.

Brad had already considered that. He knew that if he wanted his mother's cooperation, he'd have to bargain. "The pleasure of my company. I'll agree to have dinner with you once a week for the next three months if you agree to this." The few times he'd seen her since he'd moved to the boardinghouse, his mother had lamented his absence from her dinner table.

Though she looked down, as if seeking answers from the Aubusson rug, Brad could see her wavering. "Your father will never agree," she said slowly.

"I think he will if you ask him."

This time Mother fixed her stare on him. If she expected him to back down, she was disappointed. "All right," she said at last. "But there will be no second chances."

"Fair enough."

"Are you sure you know which one is the fish fork?"

If Brad hadn't been so earnest, Eleanor would have laughed at the question. But she knew his concern was for her, and that thought warmed her more than the August sun. "I do," she admitted. "My mother taught me about fish forks—and fish knives too."

It remained to be seen whether Mama's lessons and years of experience had prepared her for dinner with Brad's parents. Though the invitation had been issued by Mrs. Harrod, carefully inscribed on monogrammed stationery, Eleanor had no doubt that Brad had been the instigator. His determination to win his parents' approval seemed to be limitless, and that pleased her. She only hoped the elder Harrods were as eager to rebuild their family.

While she had no doubt her prowess with dining utensils rivaled Mrs. Harrod's, Eleanor suspected that adherence to etiquette would not be enough to convince

Brad's parents of her suitability as a daughter-in-law. Rather than burden Brad with her fears, she said lightly, "I even learned the difference between cream and clear soup spoons."

Brad cranked the motor of his Model T, then jumped in beside Eleanor, giving her an openly admiring look. "That must be because you lived in a city."

Though that was part of the reason, it wasn't relevant. Brad appeared to still harbor the same misconceptions she'd had when she first moved to Hidden Falls. She couldn't let him believe she was the only Moreland Mills employee who could face a formal dinner table with equanimity.

"You might be surprised. Many of the other mill hands had lessons in deportment. Just because they were raised on farms doesn't mean they're uncivilized." Despite the short time allocated for meals and the women's hunger, Mrs. Weld was a stickler for proper table manners and did not hesitate to correct infractions. As a result, meals at the boardinghouse could have served as models for decorum.

Brad looked abashed. "I didn't mean to imply that. I guess I'm more nervous than I realized, and my tongue wasn't attached to my brain."

Eleanor smiled at the unlikely image. "I'm the one who ought to apologize. You know I get overwrought when anyone makes general observations about the mill workers." She gave Brad a mischievous smile. "I could blame that particular propensity on the column

I'm writing for a certain paper, but that wouldn't be fair, so I'll just step down from my soapbox now."

"Shall we start over?" Brad gave her an appraising glance as they drove down Main Street. "May I say, Miss Menger, that you're looking particularly beautiful this evening?"

"Why, thank you, Mr. Harrod." Eleanor continued the mocking formality they adopted when they wanted to lighten their moods. "It's borrowed finery." Once again she had been touched by her friends' concern. When they'd heard about the invitation to meet Brad's parents, everyone had wanted to contribute something. As a result, Eleanor was wearing Deborah's best skirt, Virginia's lace shirtwaist, and Millie's crocheted gloves. Her clothing might not be as elaborate as the gowns she'd once worn, but it was a far cry from her ordinary dresses, and—if Brad's expression was to be believed— she would not embarrass him in front of his parents.

"Our house is called Rose Walk," he explained when they'd crossed the river and crested the hill. This side of the river boasted only three houses, but if the descriptions Eleanor had heard were accurate, the houses were mansions, giving the street the nickname of Millionaires' Row. Not only were the buildings larger and more elaborate than any in town, but unlike the ordinary homes which were referred to by street addresses or the owners' surnames, these had names of their own: Rose Walk, Fairlawn, and Pleasant Hill.

"Are there many roses at Rose Walk?" Eleanor asked.

Though Brad nodded, Eleanor noticed the tension in his jaw. His calm demeanor was only a pretense. Brad was as nervous about this evening as she was. "We have more roses than most botanical gardens can claim. They're my mother's passion."

Eleanor made a mental note, hoping she could find some common ground with Brad's mother. While she wasn't a gardener, her own mother had enjoyed growing flowers and had had a number of rosebushes. "What about your father? What does he care about?"

"Father?" Brad wrinkled his nose. "The railroad. Nothing else compares to that." And that, Eleanor knew from hearsay, was part of the problem. The townspeople continued to speculate on reasons why Brad had never assumed a role at the railroad. Now that he'd founded the *Herald,* many believed it had been his choice, that he'd demonstrated no interest in the family business. Eleanor doubted that.

Brad pulled into the first driveway, turning left when it forked. The right turn, Eleanor guessed, led to the stables. A few seconds later, she had her first view of Rose Walk. Deborah had not exaggerated. It was a mansion, a Georgian-style redbrick building that could easily house a dozen people.

Formal hedges lined the front walk, while a mass of petunias spilling over the edges of two large urns added color and softness to the front porch. It was a beautiful house, and yet to Eleanor, it appeared almost forbidding. Other than the petunias, everything was rigid and perfectly groomed. How had fun-loving Brad grown up here? Or was that perhaps the reason for his sense of humor? Had he developed it as an antidote to a serious household? None of those were questions Eleanor could—or would—ask.

As Brad switched off the motor and helped her out of the car, the front door opened, revealing the couple Eleanor had seen from a distance several times. Dressed in a silk gown that could only have come from Paris, Mrs. Harrod exuded quiet elegance, while the man at her side was best described as distinguished. Neither, however, could be said to be welcoming. Though they murmured the right words, their voices were devoid of warmth. Brad might have claimed otherwise, but as Eleanor had suspected, the elder Harrods had invited her under duress.

"I'm so sorry, Miss Menger," Brad's mother said when the social amenities had been observed and they were seated at the long dining table. "I forgot to ask Brad whether you ate escargots."

It wasn't a lapse of memory, Eleanor knew, but a deliberate attempt to embarrass her as she attempted to extricate the delicious morsels from their shells. The deportment lessons the other mill hands had taken would hardly have included the intricacies of eating French snails.

"Your chef is renowned," Eleanor said calmly, refusing to let the other woman win this round. "I look forward to anything he serves."

By the end of the meal, it was apparent to Eleanor, if not to Brad, that each course had been chosen with an eye to the difficulty involved in eating it. The escargots had been followed by a particularly delicate whitefish that required skill with both the fish knife and fork, while the meat course had featured a sauce that rendered it slippery. Even dessert, individual meringues with a lemon filling, provided hazards to the uninitiated. As she cleared each hurdle, Eleanor watched Mrs. Harrod's face. Not once did she let her surprise show, nor did she exchange any private glances with her husband. Though she might be testing Eleanor, she was polite enough to say or do nothing untoward.

For the most part, the dinner conversation was pleasant if superficial. They discussed the weather, the town's carousel, the next musicale. Not once, however, did either of Brad's parents mention any of his endeavors. It was as if the *Herald* and the lyceum did not exist. When Eleanor alluded to one of Brad's articles, his mother adroitly changed the subject, an act that left Eleanor fuming inwardly.

"I understand you work in the mill." Mr. Harrod addressed Eleanor for the first time after the butler removed their dessert plates.

"Yes, Mr. Harrod, I'm fortunate enough to be employed there."

"Fortunate?"

"It's one of the best mills in the country. The Moreland quality and concern about workers are well known, as is the punctuality of your railroad. I had a most pleasant journey on one of your trains."

Brad's father nodded, a king accepting his due, and

changed the subject. Half an hour later, when the conversation flagged, Eleanor gestured toward the silver bowl brimming with red and white roses. "These flowers are beautiful. The stories I've heard about your garden did not exaggerate."

For the first time, Mrs. Harrod appeared to thaw ever so slightly. "I enjoy them, although I would enjoy them more this season if I were not plagued with insects."

"Have you tried burying a banana peel next to the bush?" Eleanor asked, recalling a remedy her mother had used. "I read that that will discourage pests and provide additional nutrients for the flowers."

"Indeed? I'm not familiar with that technique, but I'll try it." The thawing seemed to increase.

When the butler had refilled their coffee cups for the third time, Brad's mother nodded slightly. "Shall we retire to the parlor?"

Brad shook his head. "I'm sorry, Mother, but I need to get Eleanor back to her boardinghouse. We have curfews, you know."

Though both parents frowned at the reminder that their son no longer lived with them, neither said anything. Instead, they rose and escorted Brad and Eleanor to the door, their farewells as correct as their welcome had been and just as cool. It was only when Eleanor was in the motorcar and Brad walked to the front to crank it that she heard his mother's voice drifting through the open window.

"At least she knew what to do with a fish fork."

Eleanor couldn't help it. She laughed.

Chapter Nine

Brad whistled as he drove toward Rose Walk. When he was alone in the car, it didn't matter that his whistling was tuneless. What mattered was expressing the joy that threatened to overflow his heart. She was wonderful! Though he longed to shout his happiness from the rooftops, or at least confide it to a friend, there was no one who'd understand. Surely no one else had ever been this happy.

Soon after his marriage, Anthony had written of a joy beyond anything he'd imagined. What Brad felt was that and more. Now that Gracie had died, it would be cruel to mention happiness to his friend. That left Charles. The problem was, Charles had always been more restrained than Anthony and had not discussed his feelings for Susannah. If Brad confided in him, Charles would smile and tell him he wasn't impartial.

Brad couldn't deny that. In his estimation, Eleanor Menger was the most wonderful woman in the world, making everyone else pale in comparison. That was another reason he couldn't talk to Charles. The man might not like knowing his sister had been eclipsed, at least in Brad's universe. And so he whistled, more loudly now that he'd crossed the river.

Was there anything Eleanor could not do? Though Brad would admit he'd been worried, it had been clear from the beginning that she'd learned a great deal from those deportment lessons her mother had insisted on. Even Brad's mother, a notorious stickler for proper etiquette, had not frowned once during the meal. Why would she? Eleanor had dealt with the complex dishes Mother had ordered as if she'd had a lifetime of practice. Not only that, but she'd managed to keep the conversation flowing with seeming ease, changing subjects as deftly as Mother did when she reached an impasse. Brad had known it would take more than one dinner to convince his parents Eleanor was the perfect woman for him, but surely that had been an auspicious beginning.

To give his parents credit, they'd kept their side of the bargain. There had been no snide comments, no overt hostility. Although the atmosphere had been a bit cool, it was not frigid. They'd done their part. Brad would do his. That was why he was on his way to the weekly dinner he'd promised.

"I heard the paper's circulation is increasing," Father said after the butler set plates of pot roast and vegetables in front of them.

Brad nodded, trying not to smile at the differences between tonight and the evening Eleanor had been a guest. Tonight's meal was far simpler than the one she had shared. Tonight there were no dishes designed to test the diner's skill with cutlery. Tonight his father was not dismissing any mention of Brad and his accomplishments. Instead, he'd introduced the subject. And, if Father's tone was any indication, he was starting to respect the *Herald*. While Eleanor might not have been directly responsible for those changes, Brad believed she'd had a role. Perhaps when his parents had seen him with her and had realized how well suited they were, they'd started to reconcile themselves to the idea of Brad as a grown man, able to make his own decisions, capable of choosing a bride as well as a career.

He didn't try to conceal his pride. "We're even shipping a few copies to major cities—New York, Boston, and Philadelphia," he told his parents. "I have to admit that surprised me. I didn't expect people there to be interested in small-town news."

His father reached for a roll. "Hidden Falls isn't an ordinary small town. Moreland Mills sees to that. I imagine some people read the paper thinking they'll get advance warning of any significant changes." Though Father's voice was neutral, the look he gave Brad said he'd raised this topic for a reason, and it wasn't necessarily one Brad would like. Brad watched as he slathered butter on the roll, took a bite, and chewed carefully before he spoke. "They may buy the paper once or twice, but I suspect they'll be disappointed when they discover the biggest news is the Independence Day celebration." Though unspoken, there was no doubt he had been disappointed himself.

Brad's earlier elation evaporated under the force of his father's disapproval. Why had he thought today would be different? Father would never change. "Nothing I do pleases you, does it?"

Father's gaze remained as rigid as the rails his trains rode. "How can I be pleased when you continue to fritter away your life on passing interests?"

"The *Herald* is not a passing interest." Brad sawed a piece of roast in a vain attempt to vent his frustration. "It may surprise you, Father," he said when he could trust himself not to shout, "but I can envision myself running the paper for the rest of my life."

His father's face flushed with anger. "What about the railroad?"

"What about it? You never wanted me to be involved. What has changed?"

The tightening of his lips was the only sign Brad's words had hit their mark. "Nothing," his father said shortly. "Nothing at all."

Brad heard a small gasp from the other side of the table. When he looked at his mother, he saw her habitual smile faltering. "Cook made the pot roast especially for you, dear," she said, gesturing toward Brad's plate. "I hope you're enjoying it." In a desperate attempt to change the subject, his mother had seized on the time-honored tradition of food.

While it was true that pot roast was one of his favorite

dishes, Brad could have been eating a Moreland Mills towel for all the flavor he tasted. "It's delicious," he lied. Then, recognizing her ploy for what it was, an attempt to restore equanimity at the dinner table, he nodded at the centerpiece of roses. "Are you still having trouble with ants?" Brad cared not a whit about the flowers. All he wanted was to finish this meal and escape. Though the boardinghouse might lack fancy rugs and fine china, it also lacked vitriolic conversation. That was a more than fair trade.

"Why, no, I'm not." The pleasure in his mother's voice told Brad she appreciated his question, even if his interest was feigned. "The ants are gone, and my roses are as healthy as I've ever seen them."

Brad managed a smile. "Then the banana peels must have worked." Though it was a minor victory, he could hardly wait to tell Eleanor that his mother had followed her advice. Eleanor was bound to ask about tonight. Now he had at least one positive thing to report.

Thanks to Mother, the rest of the meal passed uneventfully. With the skill that made her such an accomplished hostess, she kept the conversation centered on neutral topics. It was only when their coffee had been poured that Brad ventured into uncharted waters and risk another rebuff.

"We're having our second lyceum lecture next week," he said, addressing his words to both parents. "If you've read the *Herald,* you know I'll be the speaker. I hope you'll come."

Mother nodded. "We'll . . ."

"Be in New York that day." As Father completed the sentence, his mother's startled expression confirmed Brad's suspicions. This was either a lie or a sudden change of plans.

"I see." And he did. He'd been correct when he'd stated that nothing would please Father. No matter what Brad did, the man would not approve. And because he did not approve, he would do nothing that could be viewed as approbation, not even attending his son's lecture.

Brad sipped his coffee as he tried to quell his disappointment. If he'd had only himself to consider, he could have accepted his father's dismissal of his efforts. But the stakes were higher—much higher. The lecture wouldn't matter if it hadn't been the next step in convincing Father to trust his judgment and to recognize that Brad had chosen wisely when he'd asked Eleanor to marry him. If Father wouldn't support him on something as small as the lyceum, there was no hope he'd approve Eleanor as a daughter-in-law. But he had to. There was nothing more important in Brad's life. Somehow—someway—he had to change Father's opinion. If he didn't, he would lose Eleanor and their chance for happiness.

Eleanor took a seat in the last pew. Although Brad had protested, she was more comfortable there. Not only did it mean she could observe everyone as they entered and would be able to watch the audience's reaction while he spoke, but it also meant that if Brad's eyes focused on her—as they were wont to do—it would not be obvious. He would simply appear to be looking at the entire audience.

There were still ten minutes until the lecture was scheduled to begin, and the church was nearly full. Eleanor smiled with delight. Though Brad had claimed the news business was far less interesting than carousel carving, it seemed that tonight's audience would surpass the first. As far as Eleanor could tell, every one of the mill workers was here, along with most of Hidden Falls' permanent population. Charles and Susannah sat in the first pew next to Ralph Chambers, the town's attorney. The two women whom Eleanor knew only as Bird Hat and Flag Lady rounded out the first row, albeit with different chapeaus. Shopkeepers, the schoolteacher, the doctor, everyone was here, with one notable exception: Brad's parents.

Eleanor scanned the audience, hoping desperately she'd somehow missed their entrance, but she had not. Mr. and Mrs. Harrod were conspicuously absent. The story that they'd boarded the train this morning, accompanied by enough luggage for a week's journey, appeared to be true. Though she forced her lips into a polite smile, Eleanor's heart sank as she considered the enormity of Brad's disappointment. Other than the brief speech he'd given on Independence Day, this was his first foray into public speaking, and he'd wanted his parents to be there. Surely there was nothing so important in New York that they couldn't have postponed it.

Remembering how Mr. Harrod had ignored every reference she'd made to the *Herald* and the lyceum, Eleanor realized that Brad's parents' absence was probably deliberate, a public notice that the elder Harrods did not approve of their son's ventures.

"Excuse me, miss."

The woman's voice brought Eleanor back to the present.

Rising so the late arrival could take the seat next to her, Eleanor looked at the podium where Brad would stand in just a few minutes. How long would it be before he realized his parents were not here, and how would that affect him? There was nothing she could do to make his parents suddenly appear, but surely there was something she could do to assuage the pain.

"This is so exciting," the latecomer told Eleanor. "Mr. Harrod's paper is the best thing that's happened to Hidden Falls in a long time."

"Yes, it is." If only Brad's parents could understand that. If only they could accept him for himself.

Acceptance. Appreciation. Those were the keys. Eleanor settled back and tried to relax, though her mind continued to whirl as she realized how much alike she and Brad were. They both yearned for the same thing: approval. They'd found love, and it was glorious, but if they were going to be wholly satisfied, they needed more.

Brad sought his parents' approval. While Eleanor had never doubted that her parents loved and approved of her, ever since their death, though she hadn't been conscious of it, she'd longed for others to recognize and accept her for herself, not her money. That was one of the reasons why Clifford Warren's courtship had been so distasteful. He sought only her inheritance. Though unexpected, Eleanor had found the acceptance she craved here in Hidden Falls. The mill workers regarded her as one of them. Deborah and Virginia had freely bestowed their friendship on her. Most of all, Brad loved her. And not one knew or cared that she was an heiress.

Brad had not been so fortunate. Though he'd received the town's accolades for both the *Herald* and the lyceum, the most important approbation still eluded him. What would it take, Eleanor wondered, for Brad's parents to recognize that their son was a man with a life of his own and to give him the respect he deserved?

Eleanor pushed her worries firmly aside as Brad made his way to the podium. She wanted to savor every minute of his speech.

"It's a bit awkward being the host as well as the speaker," Brad said when he'd greeted the audience. "As the host of this lecture series, I'm supposed to introduce all the speakers. What should I say? Many of you know me well enough that you've counted the freckles on my face." Eleanor recognized Charles's laughter and heard the man in the row ahead of her snicker. That was perfect. Brad was starting the evening with his trademark sense of humor.

He waited until the laughter subsided. "I want to

thank those of you with good memories for not repeating stories of my sundry misdemeanors, particularly the time when I decided to emulate Tom Sawyer and convince my friends to paint all the fences"—Brad paused for dramatic effect—"red." As if in unison, the mill workers gasped, trying to imagine the town's pristine white picket fences turned crimson.

"I'd like to claim that I've learned from that and other misdeeds." Brad's voice grew serious. "The one thing I have learned is how much I love this town. This is my home, and if God is willing, it will always be my home. I want you to see it the way I do, as a wonderful place to live. That's why I founded the *Herald*." He leaned forward and grinned. "That's enough seriousness for one evening. Now let's turn to the reason you're all here. Let me show you how the paper is produced."

For the next hour Brad spoke, explaining each step of the process. He'd brought samples of a Linotype matrix, a finished type slug, and a dummy paper, circulating them through the audience as he described their functions. Though she had told Brad her role was an observer, Eleanor found herself so caught up in his speech that she forgot to watch for others' reactions. Like the rest of the audience, she was alternately intrigued and amused by his descriptions and the humorous anecdotes that laced his presentation.

When Brad finished, there was a moment of silence, as if the audience didn't want to believe he was done. That was followed by thunderous applause and even more questions than Rob Ludlow had received. By any standard, tonight's lecture was a success, or it would have been if only the elder Harrods had been here to witness their son's performance.

Eleanor waited until the crowd began to subside before she made her way slowly to the front of the church. "You were wonderful," she said softly when she reached Brad's side. There were only a few people left. Most had filed out, heading for the park and another ride on the carousel, for Charles had agreed that, until the weather turned too cool, the merry-go-round would be open after each lyceum lecture. Eleanor smiled as she continued. "I heard people saying your talk was better than Rob's."

Brad wrinkled his nose. "They must have short memories."

"Don't be so modest." Eleanor wanted him to have no time for reflection. That, and the realization that his parents had refused to support him, would come later. For the present, she wanted him to revel in the town's approval. "You're an excellent speaker. Once you started talking, you had everyone's complete attention. They listened, and they believed you." Remembering some of the speeches she'd heard in New York, Eleanor's lips twisted in a wry smile. "Why, Brad, I suspect you're wasted as a newspaperman. You could be a politician."

As she'd hoped, that elicited a smile, albeit a faint one. "Nonsense. I have enough problems with the paper. I can't imagine trying to please a group of constituents."

It wasn't, Eleanor suspected, prospective constituents

who concerned Brad. It was his parents. Though he should be basking in the satisfaction of a job well done, as she'd feared, he was brooding over their absence. Eleanor wished she could shake some sense into them. Couldn't they see what they were doing, how they were hurting their son? Of course they couldn't, for they weren't here. She was, and she hated the disappointment etched on Brad's face and the way his shoulders slumped ever so slightly. Surely there was some way to comfort him.

"I'm sorry your parents didn't come." She laid her hand on his arm, hoping the warmth of her fingers would ease his pain, as they walked toward the door.

"It doesn't matter."

"Of course it does." She couldn't let him continue to pretend he didn't care. This was like the boil her mother had once lanced, telling Eleanor that no matter how much the needle prick hurt, it was necessary to drain the poison and start the healing process. "It's natural for us to want our parents' approval, just as it's natural for them to think they know what's best for us." That was why Papa had left her money in trust until she was twenty-five; he'd wanted to protect her. Though he'd told her how proud he was of her learning and maturity, at least one corner of his mind had viewed her as a child, needing guidance.

Brad shook his head. Eleanor wasn't sure whether he disagreed with her or whether he simply wanted to end the conversation, but she knew she would not stop until she'd told him what she'd realized earlier this evening.

They'd left the church. Though Brad appeared to hesitate, Eleanor gestured toward the park. Tonight's speaker needed to be there, to accept more congratulations and answer questions. Their time alone was only a brief interlude, but she intended to use it wisely. There was still more poison to be drained.

Eleanor paused under one of the big oak trees that shaded the church. "It must be difficult for parents to admit we're grown and don't need their advice and guidance." Her father appeared to have had particular difficulty with the idea that Eleanor might not always need a male influence in her life.

"I think they fear we won't need them anymore. They seem to forget that no matter how old we are, we still need their love." Eleanor felt the tendons in Brad's arm tighten. Though he remained silent, it was clear he was not enjoying this conversation. She wasn't either, but somehow she had to make him understand.

She stopped and turned to face him. "Your parents love you, Brad." He started to shake his head. "They do," she countered. "I could see it in the way they look at you when they think no one's watching. Even their disapproval of me is part of that love. They don't want you to make a mistake that would cost you your happiness. They love you, and they want you to be happy."

Brad's lips thinned. "If that's what they're trying to achieve, they're going about it all wrong. I feel as if I'm fighting every time I'm with them. I don't like fighting, but I don't want to lose."

In the distance, the sound of the Würlitzer organ

faded, signaling the end of a carousel ride. Eleanor knew Brad should be in the park, but she couldn't let him go until they'd settled this.

"I'm sure your parents don't want to lose either. Did you ever consider that they may be afraid they'll lose your love and that's why they're fighting so hard?"

The widening of Brad's eyes was the only sign she'd surprised him. He nodded his head almost imperceptibly. "They will lose my love if they continue."

It was what Eleanor had feared, that the rift was widening. "Oh, Brad, don't say that."

"I can't help it. That's the way I feel." He stared into the distance for a moment. When his eyes met hers again, their expression was so bleak Eleanor wanted to cry. "I don't want to talk about them anymore. You're all that matters to me."

Before she knew what he intended, Brad drew her into his arms and lowered his lips to hers. This kiss was nothing like the first one. That had been sweet and tentative as they'd learned the shape and feel of each other's mouths. This one was firmer, tasting of desperation. Even the way he held her made Eleanor realize Brad was clinging to her as if to a lifeline. She'd spoken of need. At least for the moment, he needed her. Brad didn't need her approval; she'd already given that. But he did need love. Surely there was a way she could show him how much she loved him.

Slowly, Eleanor raised her hands and cupped Brad's face, letting her fingers caress his cheeks. She forced herself to move slowly, her fingers gliding over his skin, learning the contours of his face. It was a loving gesture, if only he recognized it. But the tension, the anger, and the desperation did not seem to recede. It was time for a drastic move.

Eleanor pulled her lips from his. When he murmured a protest and tried to recapture them, she shook her head.

"Trust me." Her fingers continued their exploration, reaching his forehead and gently smoothing the furrows. Playfully, she kissed the tip of his nose.

"No fair," he said, wrinkling that portion of his anatomy.

"Everything's fair." To prove it, she pressed light kisses along the edges of his mouth, dodging his attempts to kiss her.

"You're driving me crazy."

It was what she wanted. If he was concentrating on her, he couldn't be angry or hurt. Eleanor kissed Brad's chin and then his nose.

"How many freckles do you have?" she asked and began to give each one a kiss. As his lips curved into a smile, Eleanor succumbed to temptation and molded her lips to his.

Perhaps it was an hour, perhaps only a moment. All she knew was that for the space of a kiss, the man she loved seemed to be happy. For tonight, that would have to be enough.

It was Saturday afternoon, and as she often did on her shortest workday, Eleanor was shopping in the general store. Today she was looking for something special for Deborah's forthcoming trip home. Though her friend was counting the days until she'd see Franklin again, she was also haunting the post office, wondering why she hadn't heard from him. In the past, he had been a regular correspondent, with a letter arriving each Tuesday. For three weeks now, there had been no letter, despite several from Deborah, asking if he were ill, and that worried both Deborah and Virginia. Eleanor looked around the store, searching for something to help boost Deborah's spirits.

As she headed toward the display of linen handkerchiefs, the bell tinkled, signaling the arrival of another customer. Eleanor looked up, then blinked when she recognized the woman. Hadn't Brad said his mother rarely visited the Hidden Falls stores and never on Saturdays when she might encounter mill workers? But she was here and, to Eleanor's surprise, had her gaze fixed on her, almost as if she'd come in search of Eleanor. That was, of course, a preposterous thought. Mrs. Harrod didn't want to see her.

"Good afternoon, Mrs. Harrod." With the manners her mother had instilled in her, Eleanor approached the older woman. It would be unthinkably rude to ignore her. "I want to thank you again for the delicious dinner." Though she'd sent a note expressing her gratitude, Eleanor was at a loss for another topic of conversation. The one thing they had in common was Brad, but this was hardly the place to tell his mother how much he was suffering.

Mrs. Harrod appeared equally ill at ease. She pursed her lips, then nodded shortly, as if she'd made a decision. "I thought I would go to the hotel for a cup of tea before returning home. Would you care to join me?"

Her stilted words told Eleanor she was improvising. Curious about the reason for this first amicable gesture, Eleanor nodded. "Thank you. I'd enjoy that."

If Eleanor had had any doubts that this was not Mrs. Harrod's routine, the hotel maître d's expression would have quashed them. Though he recovered quickly, he was obviously startled to see Brad's mother in his establishment.

When they were seated at a table whose location at the back of the room ensured they would not be overheard, Mrs. Harrod ordered a pot of tea and a plate of sandwiches. Though her posture was as perfect as ever, she shifted in her chair, as if uncomfortable. That was a feeling Eleanor shared, wondering why this woman sought her company.

Mrs. Harrod managed a small smile. "I don't know whether my son told you, but my roses are flourishing again. Your suggestion of burying banana peels appears to have helped them."

Brad had indeed told her. According to him, that had been the only positive moment of dinner with his parents. Choosing not to reveal either point, Eleanor said, "Roses are beautiful flowers, but they're difficult to raise."

Mrs. Harrod waited until the waiter served their food

before she replied. "Roses are like children—difficult to raise, and no matter what you do, there are thorns for the unwary." She stirred sugar into her tea and took a sip. Placing the cup firmly back on the saucer, she fixed her gaze on Eleanor. "I love my son and want him to be happy. That's the reason I wanted to talk to you." She paused for a second. "If I thought you'd agree, I'd offer you money to leave Hidden Falls and never see him again."

Her words were delivered as sweetly as if she were still discussing roses, and so it took a second before their impact registered. When they did, Eleanor felt the blood drain from her face. "I would never do that!"

Mrs. Harrod considered the platter of sandwiches, placing one on her plate before she looked at Eleanor again. Her face was so like Brad's, and yet while his eyes reflected warmth and humor, his mother's were cold and calculating. She seemed to be measuring Eleanor's reaction, searching for a way to refute it. "I was afraid of that. That's what I told Jacob you would say. Whatever you see in my son, it's not his fortune."

Though she had no way of knowing it, Mrs. Harrod's words struck a sensitive chord deep within Eleanor. How well she knew what it was to be valued only for one's inheritance. It was demeaning, reducing accomplishments, talents, and everything that defined a person to nothing more than a ledger entry.

"I love Brad." Eleanor stared at the woman who'd given him life and wondered how she could believe anyone would care only for his inheritance. "You asked what I see in Brad. What I see is a kind, loving man who truly wants to make the world a better place. That's why he started the paper and why he's doing so much for the lyceum. Brad is doing what he believes is right. Whether the paper ever makes him wealthy doesn't matter to him. Or to me. I love Brad. Even more than that, I admire him, especially his ideals."

"You can't live on ideals."

"I wouldn't want to live without them." Though Mama would have been appalled by her retort, Eleanor did not regret it. Brad's mother ought to recognize how special her son was.

The tightening of her fingers on the teacup was the only sign of Mrs. Harrod's disapproval. "Miss Menger, let me be blunt," she said at last. "What would make you leave Hidden Falls?"

Nothing. But before she voiced the thought, Eleanor realized it was not true. As much as she hated the thought of leaving Hidden Falls, she would do it under the right circumstances—or, rather, the wrong ones. "There is one way I'd leave, and that's if Brad no longer loved me."

His mother sighed. This time when her eyes met Eleanor's, their expression had changed. Perhaps it was Eleanor's imagination, but she thought she saw grudging admiration. "You're as stubborn as he is."

"I'd like to say we're both determined." Eleanor sipped her tea, wondering whether she should confide in this woman. Whether or not Mrs. Harrod realized it, they both sought the same thing: Brad's happiness. "Has Brad told you that he asked me to marry him?" A nod. "Did he also tell you that I refused unless he had your approval?"

The woman's eyes widened. "No, I didn't realize that." She bit into a tiny sandwich, chewing carefully before she spoke again. "I'm curious, Miss Menger. Why would you set those conditions?"

"Because I love Brad and want him to be happy. I don't think he can be completely happy if he's estranged from you and his father."

Mrs. Harrod nodded slowly. "It seems we're agreed on one thing. However, we differ on what will bring Brad happiness."

The waiter returned with a second pot of tea. Though Mrs. Harrod appeared annoyed by the interruption, Eleanor used the delay to consider her response. This might be her one opportunity to speak with Brad's mother. She had to use it to try to make her understand all that was at stake. If the elder Harrods continued their current course, they'd lose their son as surely as if he died.

"I hesitate to say this, lest I appear rude, but Brad is no longer a child. Shouldn't he be the one who decides what will make him happy?"

A long silence greeted Eleanor's question. "It's not easy being a parent," Mrs. Harrod said at last. "We want the best for our children, but it's not always clear what that is." She fixed her gaze on Eleanor, as if trying to read her thoughts. When she spoke, her words were the last ones Eleanor had expected. "Will you join me here next week?"

It was annoying, downright annoying. Abel punched the sidewalk with his cane as he made his way to the newsstand. In the past, he had sent servants to purchase newspapers and magazines, but the servants were all gone. Despite his promises of payment, they'd left, announcing they could no longer wait for back wages. One had even had the temerity to mention that a household that could no longer afford fresh vegetables was one where he had no desire to be employed. As if a servant had any right to criticize his betters, even if his betters were going through a temporary setback.

It was all the chit's fault. Abel clenched the cane, wishing he could wield it against the little missy. If only that ungrateful wretch would return home, he would have the money he needed. All that and more. But Eleanor had not returned, and the investigator who had charged so much for his services had failed to find her.

"Got any new papers?" Abel demanded when he reached the newsstand. Though he had to curtail most expenses, this was a necessary one. In the past, the papers had led him to investment opportunities. Unfortunately, the last two investments had proven to be less profitable than he'd expected. That, combined with the absence of Eleanor's money, had created his current problem. He'd find her soon—he was certain of it—but in the meantime, he had to find a way to cover his debts. A newspaper was his best bet.

"We started getting this one." The clerk held out a paper. "It's from Hidden Falls."

Hidden Falls. Abel had heard of that town. There were big things going on there, or so he'd been told. "Okay, give me one." Grudgingly, he doled out a few coins, then turned and stomped home. This piece of newsprint had better have something worthwhile in it.

Settling in his favorite chair, Abel opened the paper and began to peruse the columns, frowning as he read the opening paragraphs. What a waste of money! Who cared that some carousel carver delivered a lecture? Who cared that the newspaper editor would speak at the next meeting? Surely no one cared that there was a new column, written by a mill worker. What an absurd idea! Everyone knew that mill workers were illiterate. Just to prove his theory, Abel started reading the column.

His eyes widened when he saw the first sentence. Was it possible? He read the sentence again, then began to chuckle. Luck was with him, indeed. This was better than an investment opportunity. Much better. An investment took time. What he'd found promised instant riches. Who would have ever imagined that this miserable excuse for reporting held the key to what he'd sought for far too long?

"The day mill workers are not an essential part of Hidden Falls will be the day the Hudson River flows north," the columnist declared in her opening paragraph. Abel's chuckle turned into a full-fledged laugh. He'd found her! There was no one else on earth who would use that annoying phrase. Just to be certain, he searched for the author's name. Though other columns boasted a byline, this one had only the author's initials. E. M. That was all he needed. E. M. was Eleanor Menger.

Abel grabbed his hat and headed for Clifford Warren's home. It was time for action.

Chapter Ten

Eleanor took a final look in the small mirror, assuring herself that her straw hat was on straight.

"Don't worry. You look beautiful." Deborah didn't bother to hide her amusement over Eleanor's primping. "Brad won't be able to take his eyes off you."

Though she was pleased that she'd been able to distract Deborah, it was the thought of Brad watching her the whole time he drove his Model T that made Eleanor chuckle. "He'd better keep his eyes on the road."

As he had the day they'd walked to the falls, Brad had insisted on their destination being a surprise. When he'd invited her to spend Saturday afternoon with him, the only thing he had told Eleanor was that they would have a picnic. She'd tried to dress accordingly, donning her dark blue skirt and a crisp white shirtwaist. And, because this was a special occasion, she had opened her trunk and brought out the one personal item she'd brought from New York: her shell necklace. Though it had small intrinsic value, the string of seashells was Eleanor's most prized possession.

"I've been counting the hours." As they left the boardinghouse, Brad took her hand in his and led her toward the motorcar.

"So have I," Eleanor admitted. In that respect, she was like Deborah. They were both conscious of time. The difference was, Eleanor had been counting the hours remaining until a happy occasion, while Deborah marked the ever-increasing time since she'd heard from Franklin. It was a critical difference. Eleanor's countdown was over. She could only hope that Monday's mail delivery would end Deborah's worries. In the meantime, while Eleanor was enjoying her free time and the chance to spend it with Brad, her friend was left to conjure reasons for her intended husband's silence.

"I hope you'll like our destination." Despite Deborah's prophecy to the contrary, Brad kept his eyes fixed on the road as they left the town limits. "It's one of my favorite spots."

Eleanor suspected she wouldn't care if they visited a rubbish heap. What mattered was being with Brad. But a lady couldn't be so forward as to state that, and so she said simply, "Will there be any berries to pick?"

Swiveling his head to look at her, Brad was unable to mask his surprise. "How did you guess?"

"You mean we are going berry picking? What fun!"

Brad wrinkled his nose as he returned his attention to

the road. "It was supposed to be a surprise. I don't know how you guessed it. I don't think I gave you any hints." A look of feigned horror crossed his face. "Oh, no! Is it possible you can read my mind?"

Eleanor shook her head, enjoying the light bantering and his carefree expression. "Your secrets are safe. I was just thinking about our walk to the falls, and that reminded me the raspberry bushes might be ripe now. That's all. Nothing mysterious." She gave him a playful smile. "I don't suppose you'll tell me what kind of berries we're going to pick."

"Of course not. A man needs to retain some element of surprise."

Eleanor settled back in the seat. Though the country-side they were passing was beautiful, its rolling hills so lush they could have been green velvet, she found her gaze moved to Brad far more often than to the pastoral landscape. The brown-and-white specks on the hills, which she knew to be dairy cows, were less alluring than the freckles on his nose and cheeks, and the warmth of the sun seemed to pale next to his smile. Though she longed to shout her happiness from the hilltops, once again, Eleanor was mindful of what a lady could and could not say.

"This is so beautiful." Lest there be any confusion, she gestured toward the verdant hills.

"I've always loved this part of the state." The smile Brad gave her was more relaxed than she'd seen in weeks, leading Eleanor to suspect he'd chosen their destination for his own sake as well as hers. He nodded a greeting as they passed a horse-drawn wagon. "I rode in one of those wagons once, although it was filled with turnips rather than watermelons." The memory was obviously a happy one, for Brad's smile broadened as he said, "My uncle used to bring me here every year, despite my parents' protests. They were convinced I'd hurt myself."

"In a berry patch?" Though she had no experience, Eleanor could not imagine what perils accompanied berry picking. Surely not even the most protective of parent worried about an occasional prick from a thorn.

Raising his eyebrow in mock severity, Brad said, "You never can tell what hazards may be lurking. I'm sure my mother pictured poisonous snakes or at least giant spiders, all waiting to attack me."

"But you escaped unharmed."

He shrugged. "Not totally. I did break my arm one year."

"In a berry patch?" What on earth had he been doing?

Brad's laugh filled the car. "I did it in the very place we're going to today." Giving her a wry smile, he said, "Forewarned is . . ."

"Forearmed?" Eleanor winced as he touched his arm. "Bad pun, Brad. Surely you can do better."

"Alas, every coherent thought flees when blinded by your beauty."

"Now you're mixing metaphors," Eleanor said with a laugh. It was so much fun, being with Brad. His outrageous words and the melodramatic tone with which he delivered them lightened her spirits and made her wish he could always be this happy.

"If you're daring to impugn my use of the English language, ignoring the fact that I am a highly respected journalist whose words enlighten an entire town's population . . ." Brad stopped, as if he'd exhausted his hyperbole. "It is time to change the subject," he announced. Clearly searching for a new topic, he turned toward Eleanor and gestured at her throat. "That's an unusual necklace."

It was unique. Though the store had carried an assortment of jewelry fashioned from seashells, no two were alike. Mama had expressed a preference for a necklace of conches alternating with scallops, but the one that had caught Eleanor's eye had boasted only a single variety of shell: the periwinkle. As carefully strung and hand-knotted as a strand of pearls, the shells formed a collar-like necklace which reminded her of Egyptian jewelry she'd seen in a museum.

She fingered one of the periwinkles. "Papa bought this for me the last time we visited Coney Island. He called it a souvenir, and it has been exactly that—a wonderful reminder of happy times." Eleanor's throat thickened as she said, "I'll always remember that day as our last perfect time as a family."

Brad's touch on her hand was light but designed for comfort. "You're fortunate you have those memories."

Fingering her necklace again, Eleanor nodded. It was true memories had gotten her through the difficult years living with Uncle Abel, and for that she was grateful. But memories were part of the past. Brad had something far more valuable. "I may have memories, but you have the present and future to spend with your parents."

Brad's carefree mood evaporated. "That's only true if I accept their terms. In their eyes, I'll always be a child."

"I think your mother is trying to change." Eleanor and Mrs. Harrod had had tea together twice now. Though the older woman had said nothing directly, Eleanor sensed she was becoming more receptive to the idea of her son as an adult, capable of making his own decisions.

"That may be, but my father is as unmovable as these hills. Even if I live to be a hundred, I'll never convince him. I don't want to wait that long, Eleanor. I love you, and I want to marry you now."

As she wanted to marry him. The difference was, Eleanor still believed his parents could be won over. Surely they were reasonable people who wouldn't willingly sacrifice their relationship with their only son. It would simply take time for them to realize that. But Brad was impatient. He had told Eleanor it was his worst flaw, a companion to his quick temper.

It was her thoughtless words that had roused his anger, strengthened his impatience, and threatened to spoil their day. With all her heart, Eleanor wished she had not mentioned his parents. But she had, and now the only thing she could do was try to mitigate her mistake.

"Even mountains move. Rain and wind, snow and ice—they all change them."

Brad's frown deepened. "That may be true, but it

takes centuries. I can't wait that long." He gripped the steering wheel, turning the motorcar onto a narrow lane, then stopping as soon as they were off the main road. "This is our day, Eleanor. Let's pretend there's no one else in the world." His voice was so serious, his expression so fierce that Eleanor wanted to cry. But maybe he was right. Maybe if they pretended, they could recapture their earlier carefree mood.

Extending her hand for a ritual shake, she said as lightly as she could, "Your wish is my command, kind sir."

Brad shook her hand, then raised it to his lips for a brief kiss. "Shall we go berry picking, milady?"

But they weren't berries at all, Eleanor discovered as they drove down the lane toward a large farmhouse. Instead, Brad had brought her to a peach orchard. Perhaps it was pretense; perhaps it was the memory of childhood visits. Eleanor didn't know the reason, and she didn't care. What mattered was that Brad had regained his sense of humor. His eyes sparkled with mischief, and his grin was as wide as ever. It was as if those few unpleasant moments had not occurred.

"This is the tree I was trying to climb when I broke my arm," he said, leading Eleanor toward the site of his downfall. "See that branch?" It was so slender Eleanor wondered how anyone—even a reckless boy—would have dared climb out on it. "That's the culprit." As quickly as it had come, his somber mood had dissipated. When he'd introduced Eleanor to the farm owners and picked up an empty bushel basket, he led her back into the orchard. "Now, Miss Menger, it's time to work for your supper."

Surely nothing so enjoyable could be called work. Although there were a number of families in the orchard, all bent on the same goal, Brad found a row of trees where no one else was picking. To Eleanor's amusement, he walked from tree to tree, touching the low-hanging fruit but pulling nothing.

"I thought we were supposed to pick peaches."

Brad grinned. "Patience, my dear. You'll be working before you know it." He held another ripe peach in his hand, carefully inspected it, then, apparently satisfied, twisted it from the tree. "First, we eat." Pulling a knife from his pocket, Brad sliced the succulent fruit and handed Eleanor a piece. "Try this," he said, his eyes sparkling with enthusiasm. "I think you'll like it."

She did. Eleanor had eaten peaches dozens of times before, but never had one tasted so delicious. Perhaps it was the fact that it was so fresh. Perhaps it was the sun-kissed warmth. Perhaps it was the fact that it was Brad who was feeding her the tasty morsels. Eleanor didn't know, and she didn't care. The fruit was wonderful; the moment was perfect; that was all that mattered.

When they'd finished eating, they worked together to pick a bushel for their boardinghouses, laughing as they debated over the merits of each individual peach, placing the selected fruits in the baskets as carefully as if they were fragile pieces of glass, singing silly songs about peach picking, all set to the tune of nursery rhymes, and—the most fun—stealing kisses when they thought no one was looking. It was hardly an efficient way to harvest fruit, but Eleanor wasn't complaining. It was fun, and for the space of an hour, Brad seemed carefree. During that hour, she caught a glimpse of the boy he'd once been, free from the constraints of home, enjoying a simpler, rural life.

With the peaches safely stowed in the car, Brad retrieved the picnic basket he'd brought and led Eleanor to a corner of the orchard. The trees were farther apart here, providing enough space to spread a blanket in their shade. Best of all, none of the other families was closeby. It was as private a spot as a public place could provide.

Eleanor settled on the blanket and smiled with pleasure. The food was ordinary—fried chicken, biscuits, and jam, accompanied by lemonade and generous servings of chocolate cake—and yet she savored it more than any meal she could recall. They spoke of ordinary things. Afterward, Eleanor could not recall a single exchange. What she did recall was how wonderful it had felt, being with Brad. More than wonderful. It had felt right, as if they had done this a hundred times before, as if they were meant to do it a thousand times more.

What a wonderful prospect that was, sharing the future with Brad. Eleanor's smile turned into one of determination. Somehow, some way she had to make that dream come true.

"I heard you and my son went peach picking." As was her custom, Mrs. Harrod waited until the waiter

..ted before she spoke of anything more seri-
..nan the weather.

"It was so much fun!" Eleanor smiled at the memory.
"I never visited a farm when I was growing up."

"That was something Brad always enjoyed as a
child." Though Eleanor had smiled, Brad's mother
frowned as she stirred sugar into her tea. "I still can't
understand the appeal. Who would volunteer to be a
common laborer in a hot and dangerous place?"

Eleanor forbore pointing out that many would describe her work at the mill in exactly those terms. The
only difference was, she was paid to be a common laborer in a hot and dangerous place. She wouldn't mention that, though, for over the past few weeks, it seemed
she was beginning to establish a rapport with Brad's
mother. Eleanor would do nothing to jeopardize that
fragile relationship. Her goal was to help Mrs. Harrod
understand her son, not remind her of Eleanor's unsuit-
ability to become his wife.

"There's nothing so delicious as a ripe peach just
plucked from the tree," Eleanor said, trying not to blush
as she recalled the kisses that had accompanied that
particular piece of fruit. "It's sun-warmed and so full of
juice you almost need a spoon to catch it all. As if that
weren't enough, there's the satisfaction of being the
one who chose it." If Brad hadn't insisted they return to
Hidden Falls, Eleanor would gladly have spent the entire day in the orchard.

"I never thought of it that way," his mother admitted.

"I rarely eat peaches. Every time I see one, I recall Brad coming home with his arm in a cast. It's probably not fair to blame the peaches, but a peach tree was the reason my boy was hurt."

Eleanor kept her eyes on the sandwich platter as she said, "I suspect he viewed the cast as a badge of honor." The truth was, after hearing Brad describe his mother's frantic reaction to a normal boyhood mishap, she was hard-pressed not to smile.

"You may be right," Mrs. Harrod conceded. "I never did hear him complain, even though I know the cast must have itched horribly. I did notice, though, that he was more careful about climbing trees after that."

The cucumber sandwich was delicious. Eleanor savored it before replying. "He made a mistake and learned from it. That's part of growing up." Giving Mrs. Harrod a wry smile, she said, "I learned about poison ivy the hard way. I have to admit that I wasn't as stoic as Brad. My poor mother had to listen to a litany of complaints. I guess I'm a bit like you and peaches. I haven't liked ivy of any kind since then." Too late, Eleanor remembered that ivy festooned one whole side of the Harrods' home.

"I hope you don't expect me to have the gardener rip it all off the house before your next visit."

Next visit? Eleanor tried to mask her surprise. As calmly as if she were discussing the frosting on the tea cakes, Mrs. Harrod continued. "I would like you to join us for dinner the next time Brad comes. I think it's time Jacob got to know you better."

...ot be a miracle, but to Eleanor's mind, it
~ next best thing.

Brad took a deep breath, trying to calm his nerves.
Was this how the gladiators felt when they were sent
into the arena to fight the lions? Or was it unarmed
slaves who were sent to battle the lions? It made no difference. Today was Brad's turn. Though he wasn't fighting a physical battle, he felt his arm muscles tighten, as
if preparing to throw a spear, and his legs seemed ready
to charge forward against the enemy. Only it wasn't an
enemy he would face. It was the man he'd always admired more than anyone else in the world.

"Hello, Father." Brad closed the office door behind
him. The battle was about to begin. Only, if Eleanor
was correct, it might not be a battle. It might be a new
beginning. Though the picnic in the orchard had been
wonderful, Brad had been unable to forget Eleanor's
expression when she spoke of her parents and how she
was left with only memories. She was right. So was
Charles, when he urged Brad to mend his relationship
with his father. He didn't want to have the same regrets
Charles did, and he didn't want to be left with nothing
but memories, particularly when the memories of these
past few months were so unpleasant.

Father would not take the first step. Though he
wished it were different, Brad had accepted that and began to plot a strategy for winning his father's approval.
He would be rain, wind, snow, and ice all at once. The
first part of his strategy was choosing time and location.

Time was easy: Brad couldn't afford to wait. As for location, it wasn't difficult to decide that the best place for the discussion was his father's office. Perhaps if Father were on comfortable ground—his own territory, as it were—he would be more amenable.

"To what do I owe the honor of this visit?"

Though there was no hint of warmth in his father's voice, Brad resisted the urge to retaliate with caustic words. They would accomplish nothing other than deepen the rift between them. "I'd like to talk to you." He settled into the chair on the opposite side of the desk, despite the lack of an invitation.

"If it's about that girl . . ."

Once again, Brad forced back anger. "Her name is Eleanor," he said as mildly as he could. "And, yes, she's part of what I want to discuss, but only part." He took a deep breath, steeling himself for his father's reaction to his next words. "I want to talk about you and me."

"What about us?" For the first time, curiosity tinged his father's voice. Surely that was a good sign.

Brad had spent hours trying to find the right phrases. He'd agonized over the best way to open the discussion. He'd believed he was prepared, but faced with the reality of his father, every carefully planned word vanished. Instead of an eloquent introduction, he blurted out, "I don't know why things went wrong, why I stopped being a son you were proud of."

Both eyebrows shot up. "I've always been proud of you."

That was not the response Brad had expected. For

his father was reluctant to admit the truth, even to himself. "Excuse me for saying this, I don't think that's true." In the weeks since he'd moved out of Rose Walk, Brad had spent hours thinking about his father, trying to pinpoint the timing and the cause of their rift. He believed he'd found the time. The cause eluded him. "When I look back on it, everything seemed to change the first year I went away to school."

Father picked up his pipe and began to clean it. It was, Brad knew, a delaying tactic. Though his father rarely smoked, when he wanted time to think, he would pretend to be preparing his pipe. Without looking up, he said, "You changed."

Of course he had. "That's only natural. It was the first time I was away from home." College had brought new freedoms at the same time that it had introduced new responsibilities. Thrust into a strange environment, Brad had had to make more decisions than ever before. At times he'd found that difficult; at other times, he'd reveled in his independence.

Father tapped the pipe on the edge of the trash basket, dumping the used tobacco. "I don't think you ever realized how difficult that time was for your mother. She was lonely without you."

Something in his voice and the fact that he refused to make eye contact told Brad it had also been a lonely time for his father. He blinked, and a lump formed in his throat. Odd how he hadn't considered that possibility. He'd been in a new place, exhilarated by new experiences, almost every minute of the day filled with activities. There had been little time to think about what he'd left behind. His parents' lives would have been different. There was nothing new for them, nothing to fill the void his absence had created. Brad's visits had been infrequent, and when he'd come back . . . He swallowed deeply, trying to dislodge a lump as he recalled the times he'd returned to Hidden Falls.

"When I came home for the holidays, I spent more time with my friends than with you," he said, wincing at the memory.

This time Father looked at him, his expression grim. "We realized you'd outgrown us. We were no more important to you than last year's boots."

The accusation stung. "That's not true!"

"You wanted honesty. You got it." Father's voice was little more than a snarl. "If the truth hurts, consider how much your behavior hurt your mother and me."

What had he done? Brad loved his parents. He always had. He would never knowingly hurt them, and yet somehow he had. He closed his eyes for a second as memories of the first Christmas home from college raced through his mind. His mother had asked him to accompany her on a shopping excursion, but he had refused, certain he would be bored. Brad flinched as the next vignette unfolded. Unless his memory was tricking him, Father had invited him to join him here in his office, saying there were some things he wanted to discuss with him. Once again, Brad had cried off, preferring to go ice skating with Charles. Dimly he recalled seeing pain in his father's eyes. It had been replaced so

.her's normal stoic expression that Brad
.ssed it as his imagination.

￼ took a deep breath, trying to quell the horrible
sinking feeling in the pit of his stomach. Why hadn't he
remembered the invitation and Father's reaction to his
refusal? For years, Brad had told himself that Father
had never made an overture toward him, but had deliberately excluded him from everything related to the
railroad. If he was right, his father had tried, but—faced
with Brad's rebuff—had chosen not to risk further rejection. Was that the moment when everything had
started to go wrong?

Brad looked at his father. Perhaps it wasn't too late
to undo the damage. "I must have hurt you and
Mother," he said humbly. "I'm sorry." Why hadn't he
seen that his brash behavior could have been construed
as a lack of interest? Perhaps Father had reacted like a
wounded animal, striking back at the source.

"I never meant to cause either of you pain. All I can
say is that I was so caught up in my own life that I
didn't think about anyone else." Brad stretched a hand
across the desk, hoping against hope that his father
would accept it along with his apology. "I'm more
sorry than I can say that I hurt you and Mother."

His father looked at the hand but did not touch it.
Though his instinct was to retract it, Brad did not.

"John Moreland used to tell me children were like
birds. He claimed you have to let them leave the nest."
Father stared at the wall, his expression grim. "That
was easy for John to say. He had three children."

"And you had only me, disappointing Brad."

The look his father gave Brad was filled with accusation. "You made it clear you couldn't wait to get back to college and the big city life you enjoyed so much. I knew you'd never be happy living here, so there seemed no point in giving you any responsibility at the railroad."

Seen from that perspective, Father's actions had been logical. But why hadn't he given Brad another chance? "Moving away was a passing fancy."

The response came back with the speed of a rifle shot. "Like so many of your ideas."

It was futile. His father would never touch his hand, and so Brad pulled it off the desk. Perhaps he should simply leave, admitting that their differences were irreconcilable. But he couldn't, not until he pled his case. Eleanor was right. Family was important, and Brad had to do everything in his power to restore his, for family would form the foundation of his marriage.

He waited until his father met his gaze again before he spoke. "Did you ever think I might have felt rootless because you didn't trust me to work here?"

Father's eyes widened with surprise. "Is that what happened, son? Did my actions drive you away?"

The lump that had lodged in Brad's throat began to dissolve. It had been years since his father had called him "son," years since he'd heard his voice crack. He nodded slowly. Though his next words might hurt his father, they needed to be spoken. "I thought I could never satisfy you, so I stopped trying."

There was a long silence, marked only by the ticking of the clock. At last his father said, "It seems we've both made mistakes."

The lump was gone now, replaced by an unexpected sense of exhilaration. No matter how today ended, he and Father were talking—really talking—to one another, and that was wonderful. "I hope I've learned from my mistakes." To Brad's surprise, his words came out with more force than he'd intended. "You were right in saying I wasn't always certain of what I wanted in life." His father inclined his head, acknowledging the inherent apology. "I am certain now. There are two things that I want. I want to create the best possible newspaper for this town, and I want to marry Eleanor." Brad fixed his eyes on his father, willing him to understand. "I would like your approval and Mother's, but I'm determined to do both, with or without that."

"I could make your life difficult."

The brief sense of exhilaration faded. Nothing had changed. This was the man Brad knew so well, the businessman who ruled by threats.

"You could," he admitted, "but that won't stop me." Today had been a turning point. Brad understood his father better than ever before. He recognized his own faults, and he'd vowed to try not to repeat his mistakes. But he'd also realized that nothing—not even his father's wrath—would keep him from reaching his goals. "My love for Eleanor is stronger than anything you can do."

Brad waited for the explosion. Instead, a smile softened his father's face. Brad stiffened. "I wasn't aware that I'd said anything amusing."

"I wasn't laughing at you, son. The fire in your eyes reminded me of myself when I was courting your mother." Father rose from his chair and walked toward Brad. "I'm proud of you. For the first time, I think you really do know what you want." He extended his hand and clasped Brad's as he said, "Marry Eleanor. You have my blessing."

Chapter Eleven

Eleanor had never seen Brad like this. It wasn't simply the fresh haircut or the new tie. It wasn't even the grin that seemed to reach both ears. What astonished her was that somehow he appeared to be both relaxed and excited at the same time. That shouldn't have been possible, but it was. She, on the other hand, was dominated by only one emotion: nervousness. The prospect of dinner at Rose Walk with Brad's parents did not relax her, far from it. And so she searched for other thoughts to occupy her mind.

"You look different," she told Brad as he helped her into the motorcar.

He feigned a tug at an imaginary forelock, as if he were a medieval serf, paying obeisance to his lady. "Aw, shucks, ma'am." His drawl transformed him from a serf into a caricature of a field hand. "You're gonna make me blush. A man ain't supposed to do that—'spe-cially not a man with orange hair and freckles. That would be downright ugly."

As she was intended to, Eleanor laughed. Settling back into the seat, she realized Brad had used humor to deflect her question. For some reason, he did not want to talk about whatever it was that was making him look so different.

He climbed into the car and started the motor. "I see you're wearing your shells again." No doubt about it. Brad wanted to change the subject.

"Do you think they're too informal?" Normally Eleanor would not have worn a shell necklace to din-ner, but today it was her talisman, her reminder that happy families did exist. The necklace made her feel loved, and she needed that, plus every ounce of courage she could muster to face Brad's parents again. Though his mother had seemed friendlier each time they'd met for tea, Mr. Harrod was an unknown quantity. Accord-ing to Brad, he was implacable, an unmovable barrier to their happiness.

"Your necklace is perfect, just like you." Brad flashed her a warm smile as they headed up the hill to-ward his parents' home. "Don't worry. Today will be different."

It already was, for they were meeting the older Har-rods for the Sunday noon meal rather than an evening dinner. Brad had assured Eleanor that Sunday dinner was less formal, in part because many of the servants had the day off. That was good, but the more important question, the one which caused Eleanor's heart to pound, was whether her hosts' attitude would have changed.

"It'll be all right," Brad said, giving her hand a brief squeeze as they pulled into the driveway.

Eleanor wished she shared Brad's confidence. Inside her gloves, her hands had begun to perspire, and her heart continued to race. Brad wanted—he needed—his parents' love and approval. Would he instead be faced with cold disdain? Eleanor said a silent prayer that that would not happen and that today would be different.

When they climbed out of the car, it appeared Brad was right. Today was different. As they had the last time, his parents met Brad and Eleanor at the front door. This time, though, they were smiling. Unlike the almost frigid smiles she'd seen the last time, these were genuine. Though Eleanor had no idea what had caused the change, her tension melted under the warmth of Mrs. Harrod's smile, and when Mr. Harrod extended his arm to escort her into the dining room, she felt as if she were a welcome guest.

Dinner too was vastly different. Devoid of complex dishes designed to trap an unwary guest, Eleanor had the sensation of being party to a simple meal *en famille,* complete with comfortably ordinary conversation. Mrs. Harrod spoke of her roses, while Brad's father related his pleasure that the train's passenger traffic had increased recently. Today, he told Brad with a proud smile, the owner of the livery mentioned a stranger who had hired a horse and carriage, saying he was considering moving to Hidden Falls and wanted to explore the area. Curious, the livery owner asked how the man had heard of the town and learned it was through the *Herald*.

"You're helping put us on the map, son." The statement was simple, delivered without fanfare, but the smile on Brad's face told Eleanor how much his father's praise meant to him. It was clear something had changed between the two men. The barely veiled contempt she'd seen the last time was gone. Even the way Mr. Harrod had addressed Brad as "son" was a marked change. There'd been genuine affection in his voice. Eleanor's heart soared as she realized that somehow Brad and his father had reconciled their differences. Who said miracles didn't happen? The reconciliation with his parents must be the reason Brad seemed at ease today.

Eleanor found herself anxious for the meal to end so she could ask Brad how he'd achieved so much in such a short time. It was only a little over a week since he'd declared his father to be an impenetrable, immovable obstacle. But, though the meal was less elaborate than the last time, service was leisurely, and it seemed as if hours had passed before it was time for dessert.

When the dinner plates were cleared, Eleanor looked across the table, trying to catch Brad's eye. Did he also long for some time for them to be alone? He did not meet her gaze. Instead, he stared at the table, his hand gripping the stem of the water goblet so tightly Eleanor feared he could crack it. What was wrong? He had seemed so relaxed and happy. Now he was nervous. It made no sense. His mother was speaking of a party she and Mr. Harrod would attend in Philadelphia. Surely that was no reason for Brad to be tense.

The door swung open as the butler entered the dining room with dessert. To Eleanor's surprise, instead of a tray with individual servings, he was carrying a complete cake. Making no move to cut it, the butler placed the cake and the serving utensils in the center of the table, then left. Eleanor looked at Brad again. In her family, the only reason to deviate from the custom of having all courses served was a special occasion. What could this be? She knew it wasn't Brad's birthday, and if it were one of his parents', it was odd that she was here. As cordial as they'd been today, she was still virtually a stranger to them.

A sudden silence filled the room as both parents turned toward Brad, almost as if they expected him to say something. Lifting his glass with a hand that appeared to be shaking, he took a sip of water, then rose to his feet. He looked from his mother to his father before turning his attention to Eleanor. Once again his face was serious, the freckles vivid against the unnatural pallor of his cheeks. Though his expression remained solemn, his eyes blazed with an emotion Eleanor had seen before. This was how Brad had looked when he'd asked her to marry him. But surely that wasn't what he intended. Not here, not now.

He cleared his throat and smiled at her. "I've heard

that three is a lucky number. I hope so." Though the smile he gave Eleanor radiated love, it also bore more than a hint of nervousness. She returned the smile, wanting to reassure him but not certain why he needed that reassurance. In response, Brad's smile widened. "I asked you a very important question twice before, and both times you gave me an answer I didn't like. I hope today will be different."

Eleanor's cheeks flushed with confusion and embarrassment. There was only one thing Brad could mean: marriage. He'd said he wouldn't give up, that he'd keep asking her until she agreed. Eleanor had known he was persistent, but surely he did not intend to propose marriage here with his parents as an audience. An offer of marriage was supposed to be private, a special moment shared only by the happy couple. It was true her uncle had been present when Clifford Warren had demanded her hand in marriage, but Brad was nothing like Mr. Warren. Though the settings he'd chosen before had been unconventional, they'd been private. This was not.

Eleanor looked up at Brad, trying to understand. She'd given him her answer before, a conditional acceptance, as it were. Had those conditions been met? Was that the reason he seemed so different? Had his parents given their permission?

Brad smiled, as if he'd read her thoughts. "Before I ask you the all-important question, I want to ask my parents one." He gave each of them a long, searching look. "You both know that I love Eleanor and want to marry her. If she does me the very great honor of accepting my proposal, will you welcome her into the family and treat her like a daughter?"

There was no hesitation. Mrs. Harrod nodded. "I've always wanted a daughter. Eleanor will make a fine one."

"Certainly, son. If you love her, that's good enough for me."

Joy rushed through Eleanor's veins, filling her with its warmth. Who said miracles didn't happen? No wonder Brad looked so happy and relaxed. This was what she had hoped for. Though she didn't know how it had happened, he had reconciled his differences with his parents. They were once again a family.

Brad reached for her hand. "Eleanor, will you . . ."

"Bradley!" His mother's voice registered shock and horror.

"Your mother is right." Mr. Harrod shook his head, his earlier smile transformed into a frown. "Even I know this is not the proper place to pose such a personal question."

"Brad, dear, why don't you and Eleanor visit the rose garden?" his mother suggested. "We can have our cake when you return."

To Eleanor's surprise, Brad chuckled and grinned at his parents. "That was exactly what I planned to say when you interrupted," he informed them. With a wry smile, he turned to Eleanor. "Would you like to see my mother's flowers? They're famous throughout Hidden Falls."

Not trusting herself to speak, Eleanor rose and placed

her hand in his. If he noticed that her hand was shaking, Brad said nothing. Silently, he led her out of the house to the back yard. The gardens were undeniably beautiful. Tall privet hedges provided both privacy and a backdrop to the riot of color, while flagstone paths meandered among beds filled with roses in every shade of red, pink, white, and yellow.

Eleanor took a deep breath, as much to settle her nerves as to savor the heady fragrance. Perhaps on another day she could enjoy the floral beauty. Today she had only one thought. Though she knew what Brad would ask her and how she wanted to reply, she couldn't begin their life together with a lie. Brad hated deceit. How then would he react to what she had to tell him? There was only one way to know. The moment of reckoning had arrived.

Eleanor felt the warmth of Brad's hand clasping hers. She heard the song birds' melodic trills forming a counterpoint to her and Brad's footsteps. Her nostrils filled with the scent of roses. It was a moment to cherish, or it would be if Brad was not angered by her revelation.

He led her to an ornately carved stone bench which occupied one corner of the garden. Gently disentangling his hand from hers, he gestured to Eleanor to sit, then bent one knee and reached for her hand again. His lips curved into a smile and his eyes sparkled as he began to speak. "You know I love you. There is nothing I want more than to spend the rest of my life with you. Will you make me the happiest man on earth? Will you marry me?"

It should have been easy to say yes. It was what she wanted to do, and yet . . . "Oh, Brad, I love you so much." Eleanor heard the hesitancy in her voice and saw Brad's eyes darken with surprise. "I want to marry you, but . . ." She tugged his hand, then patted the bench. This was not a time for bended knees.

"I don't understand. You sound as if you're going to refuse . . . again." Eleanor hated hearing the pain in his voice. Even more, she hated the fact that she'd been the one who put it there. "What's wrong?" he asked. "I did everything you asked. I made peace with my parents."

"And I'm so thankful you did. All three of you looked like new people today. You're a real family again, and that's important." The afternoon air was sweet, but Eleanor barely noticed. "The problem isn't you. It's me. I can't start our marriage with a lie."

Brad's gasp was audible. "What do you mean? What would be a lie?"

"Me. I'm not the woman you think I am."

One hand reached out to cup her chin, turning her so he could look into her eyes. The sparkle was gone from his, replaced by concern and confusion. "You're scaring me, Eleanor. How can you not be the woman I know and love?"

"Because I've been living a lie, and I know you hate lies."

He swallowed deeply, tightening his grip as he asked, "Were you lying when you said you loved me?"

"No, never!" She saw him begin to relax and hoped that wouldn't change when he heard the rest of her story. While it was true she'd committed no crimes, deceit was deceit, and—like Brad—she'd been taught that it was wrong.

"I love you, Brad. Please don't doubt that. The problem is, I haven't told you or anyone in Hidden Falls the truth about me. I haven't liked that. In fact, I've hated the half-truths and the way I led you to believe things that weren't accurate, but I thought it was the only choice I had."

The tick at the corner of his mouth betrayed Brad's tension. "I let everyone believe I was the penniless daughter of a shopkeeper. I'm not. The truth is, my father was a wealthy investor. On my next birthday, or sooner if I marry, I'll inherit a substantial sum of money."

Brad's hand dropped, and he stared at her, as if trying to reconcile her words with the Eleanor he thought he knew. "Was this all a game?" he demanded. "Some kind of bet with a friend?"

Eleanor shook her head. "It was no game."

"Then why did you come here? Why are you working at the mill if you don't need the money?"

"I do need the money. My uncle—he's my guardian—wanted me to marry a man I despise." Eleanor shuddered, thinking of Clifford Warren. "When I refused, Uncle Abel stopped my allowance and said he'd no longer provide food or shelter. Unfortunately, under the terms of my father's will, he could do that."

Brad's lips tightened with anger. Eleanor could only hope that anger was not directed at her.

"Uncle Abel thought I'd capitulate, but I wouldn't. Nothing, absolutely nothing on earth will make me marry Mr. Warren." She looked at the face she loved so dearly, hoping Brad understood, hoping he wasn't hurt by the deception. "I did the only thing I could think of. I needed money, and I didn't want to be near either Uncle Abel or Clifford Warren, so I left New York and came here. The mill gave me a way of earning a living until my birthday."

Brad's eyes darkened again. "Oh, Eleanor," he said, exhaling deeply. "Why did you think that would change the way I feel about you? I love you. You, Eleanor, not your money or your social standing."

"Then you don't mind that I pretended to be someone I wasn't?"

He shook his head slowly. "I wish you'd been able to trust me sooner, but I understand."

The hope Eleanor had nurtured so carefully began to grow. This was what she'd longed for, a man who loved her for herself. Brad cupped her chin again, his eyes seeming to ask whether she believed him. "If I didn't know it was impossible to love you any more than I did five minutes ago," he said, his voice husky with emotion, "I'd tell you that your revelations only increased my love. And no, my darling, I'm not talking about the fact that you're an heiress. I'm referring to your strength and determination."

His fingers moved slowly, caressing her cheek, reminding Eleanor of the evening she'd used a similar gesture to comfort him. "I know how difficult a mill worker's day is." Brad accompanied his words with a wry smile. "Your articles taught me that. After I read them, I wondered how anyone could survive a day at the mill." Though he lowered his hand, he kept his gaze fixed on her. What she saw was love and something else. Perhaps it was admiration, for his next words were, "I truly don't know how you did it. Mill work must have been especially difficult for you. After all, farmers' daughters are accustomed to physical labor, but you weren't, and yet you never complained."

Reaching for her hands, Brad clasped them between his. "I once thought I could be like one of those knights in shining armor we've all been taught about. I imagined you as a damsel in distress and pictured myself rescuing you. Now I know you don't need rescuing. I thought I could shower you with worldly goods. Now I know you don't need them. That doesn't leave me much to offer you. All I have is my love."

Before she could speak, he asked, "Is that enough? Will you marry me?"

Eleanor smiled at the man she loved so dearly. "Love is all I want or need." Threading her fingers through his, she pronounced the words she'd wanted to utter for so long. "Yes, my love, I will marry you."

When he drew her into his arms and kissed her, Brad's was a kiss of joy, of promise and of relief. Later, much later, when they'd exhausted their words of love and exchanged dozens of kisses, he led Eleanor back into the house.

"Mother and Father," he said to his parents, who

were still sitting in the dining room, the uncut cake in front of them, "I'd like you to be the first to know. Eleanor has agreed to be my wife."

"Good work, son." His father nodded approval.

Mrs. Harrod rose and hugged Eleanor. "Welcome to the family, my dear."

It truly was the most perfect of days.

Still giddy with happiness, Eleanor entered the boardinghouse, eager to share her news with Virginia and Deborah. After they'd tasted the cake and spent a pleasant hour in the Harrods' parlor, Brad had announced there was one more celebration. Their engagement, he told Eleanor, would not be official unless they shared a ride on the carousel. One ride became two, then three, until Eleanor feared she'd grow dizzy. And so, reluctantly, they'd driven back to their boardinghouses, knowing the separation would be temporary. Within a month, they'd be married and sharing their own home.

But first there were plans to make and people to tell, starting with Deborah and Virginia. Though her marriage would mean that she'd leave the mill, Eleanor knew her friendship with the sisters would continue, and she wanted them to be the first to know of her engagement.

She pushed open the door, startled to see half a dozen women congregated in the dining room. Normally at this time on a Sunday, the room was empty. A quick glance told Eleanor Virginia and Deborah were part of the group, and she moved toward them, drawn by Deborah's carefree laughter. It had been weeks since Deborah had sounded so happy.

"Oh, there you are." Deborah's smile widened when she spotted Eleanor. "Come over here. I have the most wonderful news."

Eleanor matched her friend's smile, realizing only one thing could bring her such happiness. "You received a letter from Franklin."

"Not just a letter, a love letter." The words tumbled out in a torrent. "It was a big mix-up. Somehow my letter got stuck to one of Helen's," she said, referring to a woman who lived in the other women's boardinghouse. "She's been gone for two weeks and didn't get back until this afternoon. As soon as she found the mistake, she brought the envelope right over." Deborah sighed with pleasure. "Oh, Eleanor, Franklin says he misses me so much. You and Virginia were right. There was no reason to worry. He loves me."

Deborah's face, which had been pale and serious for far too long, was flushed with happiness. "Of course Franklin loves you," Eleanor said as she hugged her friend. Her own news could wait. Tonight was Deborah's night, and rather than upstage her, Eleanor would say nothing about her engagement. Tomorrow would be soon enough.

"Franklin would be a fool not to love you," she continued, reveling in the sight of Deborah's happiness. "Now, tell me everything he said. Everything you can tell me without making me blush, that is." Eleanor settled into the chair next to Deborah and listened as her friend recounted the details of her letter. Only when a new group of women joined them and Deborah had a new audience did Eleanor rise. As happy as she was for her friend, she craved a moment or two alone, time to savor her own joy.

She stood by the staircase for a moment, as she thought about retreating to the room she shared with Virginia and Deborah. Though she'd have privacy there, the prospect of being indoors held no appeal. Eleanor smiled as she realized there was a better place. Moving quickly, she let herself out the front door. Though dusk was approaching, she had a few minutes of daylight left. She couldn't return to the place she'd first met Brad, the train, but she could spend the last minutes of this wonderful day sitting on the grass, re-membering all the moments she'd shared with him, starting with the day he'd discovered her there.

Brad. Wonderful, wonderful Brad. The man she loved. The man who, by some miracle, loved her. Eleanor touched her necklace, wishing her parents were here to share her happiness. As the familiar longing filled her, she remembered her mother saying, "Never doubt that everything happens for a reason." At the time, Eleanor had been crying over some disappointment. She couldn't recall the details; all she remembered was that it had seemed overwhelming. Mama had led her to the sofa and had wrapped her arms around her, drying her tears and trying to comfort her. Though she hadn't truly be-lieved the words, Mama's love had assuaged Eleanor's pain.

She closed her eyes for a second as memories flashed through her mind. Her parents' deaths. The unhappy years in Uncle Abel's house. His insistence that she marry Clifford Warren. They were all part of the path that had led her to Hidden Falls and Brad. Eleanor fingered the periwinkle shells, remembering the day Papa had bought it, smiling as she remembered the love he and Mama had given her, love that one day she would pass on to her child.

She was still smiling as she rounded the corner of the building. The light breeze she and Brad had enjoyed in his mother's rose garden had become a wind. Eleanor reached up to secure her hairpins.

The grass muffled his footsteps. The wind masked other sounds. She had no warning. One second she was walking. The next a man grabbed her from behind, one arm snaking around her waist and pulling her against him, while a rough hand covered her mouth. For a second, Eleanor was paralyzed with shock. This couldn't be happening.

And then he spoke, his words sending chills of fear down her spine. "You won't run away this time, Missy."

Chapter Twelve

M̲r. Warren! Eleanor's head began to reel as stars danced before her eyes. How on earth had Clifford Warren found her? She forced herself to breathe, though it was difficult with his hand clamped over her mouth. What was he doing in Hidden Falls? How had he learned she was here? Eleanor dismissed her questions. How Mr. Warren had found her was unimportant. What mattered was getting away from him. She twisted violently, trying to break his hold.

"None of that, Missy." His voice was as harsh as she remembered, a fitting companion to his bony hands. Those hands might be thin, but their underlying power surprised her. Mr. Warren had easily quashed her attempt to break away merely by tightening his grip. Virginia and Deborah had been right. Even the strength she'd developed working at the mill was no match for this man.

"You and I've got an appointment," he told her. "From what I hear, the man doesn't like to be kept waiting. He charges more if his clients are late."

Appointment? Clients? He was making no sense. Eleanor's fears intensified. A bad situation had become worse. Much worse, for she was dealing with a man who was at least a little touched in the head. There was no way to reason with someone like that. Not that she could do much reasoning with her mouth covered, anyway.

Eleanor looked around. When she saw Brad's car parked next to his boardinghouse, a glimmer of hope beckoned. Perhaps he would look out one of the windows. He'd told her he liked to do that, hoping for a glimpse of her. But the windows were dark with no sign of watchers behind the curtains. Eleanor's hope faded, then winked out as she realized her own boardinghouse had no windows on this side. No one could see her and her struggles.

As if she weighed little more than a feather pillow, Mr. Warren was propelling her forward. Her eyes darted from side to side, searching for someone to help her. Save for the horse and carriage that stood a few yards away, the street was deserted. Unfortunately, that was not unusual for this time of the day. Even if she could scream, there was no one to hear her.

Eleanor's palms grew damp at the same time her mouth grew dry with fear. Her struggles told her she could not loosen his grip, but she had to. She had to escape. The alternative was unthinkable. *Stay calm,* Eleanor told herself. That was what Deborah and Virginia had emphasized when they'd shown her ways to foil attackers. *Take them by surprise,* they had advised. It was her only hope, for with each step, Mr. Warren brought Eleanor closer to the carriage. Once inside, her chance of escape would plummet.

Though she'd been fighting him, keeping her arms and legs so rigid that he had to practically carry her, Eleanor allowed her limbs to soften. She began to walk on her own, her shoulders slumped as if she were resigned to her fate. Behind her, she felt her captor begin to relax as well. *Perfect!* Eleanor took a few more steps, baiting the trap she'd set. Abruptly, she stopped. Then, with all the force she could muster, she stomped on Mr. Warren's foot.

"Ow!" As the pain ricocheted through him, he loosened his grip. That was all she needed. Eleanor broke loose and began to run. She was free! In a moment she'd reach the boardinghouse and safety. Adrenaline rushed through her, lending her feet more speed than she'd ever known. Soon! Another few yards. She was close. She could make it. She heard Mr. Warren behind her, muttering words that would have made her mother blush. He wouldn't catch her. She would reach the house. She had to. Though Eleanor's legs ached and her breathing was ragged, she could do it. She could. She would.

Whoosh! Her breath escaped as she tumbled to the ground face first, jarring every inch of her body, the impact sending pain radiating through her. The shove had come with no warning, giving her no chance to break the fall. Her jaw had taken the worst of it, and she was aware of a pain in her chest, where her necklace dug into tender skin. The pain would fade. Eleanor knew that. But nothing could change the fact that Mr. Warren had caught her.

"You'll pay for that, Missy." He wrenched her arms behind her in a painful grasp, then yanked her to her feet. "Once you're mine, you'll see what happens to people who try to defy me."

Before Eleanor could reply, he stuffed a handkerchief in her mouth. "Women are like children," he said with an evil smile. "They're supposed to be seen but not heard."

As if she were a child, he lifted her into his arms and carried her toward the buggy. When he tossed her inside, slamming the door behind her, he added, "Don't waste your energy trying to escape. The doors are locked."

At first all Eleanor could do was try to clear her head. He'd thrown her in with so much force that she'd landed against the opposite door, a door that was indeed wedged closed. Taking a deep breath, she forced herself to sit up as she heard Mr. Warren climb onto the driver's seat. A second later, they were moving. Eleanor's heart sank as she considered her predicament. The doors were secured from the outside. Though each side of the carriage had a window, he'd not bothered to close them. There was no need, for they were far too small for her to climb out. She could scream now that she had removed the gag. But screaming would be for naught with no one to hear her.

The prospect was grim. Eleanor was stuck inside this

carriage, being driven to God only knew where by a madman. She bit back tears of frustration. Crying accomplished nothing. It would only muddle her brain, when she needed to keep it clear. *Think, Eleanor,* she admonished herself. *There must be something you can do.* But it was difficult to think with her head throbbing and her wrists burning from the rough treatment. Eleanor rubbed her wrists, hoping to ease the pain, and as she did, she glanced down. Her eyes narrowed, considering the possibilities.

Refusing to admit there was only a faint chance her plan would work, Eleanor reached for her necklace.

She was the most wonderful woman on earth, and she had promised to be his wife. How fortunate could one man be? Brad knew he was grinning like a circus clown, but he didn't care. Even a smile as big as the moon could only begin to express his feelings. The woman he loved loved him. She had agreed to marry him. As if that weren't enough, her tale had revealed her to be even more special than he'd known. What a day it had been!

He'd wandered aimlessly for an hour after he'd taken Eleanor back to her boardinghouse, trying to dissipate some of the energy that surged through him. Though he'd walked so quickly that he was almost running, he had failed. His thoughts still raced; his heart still soared with happiness and more than a little sense of wonder. Today had been the best day of his life. He couldn't let it end without seeing Eleanor once more. Perhaps if he did that and assured himself that he hadn't imagined that she'd agreed to marry him, he'd be calm enough to sleep tonight.

Filled with a new purpose, Brad turned abruptly, re-tracing his steps as he strode down Main Street toward Eleanor's boardinghouse.

"May I speak with Eleanor for a minute?" he asked when Mrs. Weld opened the door.

The housemother gave him a long look. "It's past time for callers, you know." Though not unfriendly, she gave no sign she knew he and Eleanor were engaged to be married. Was it possible Eleanor had told no one? She'd seemed eager to confide in the Sempert sisters. Though he told himself it was irrational, Brad could not dismiss the fear that he'd imagined everything.

"It'll only take a minute. Please, Mrs. Weld."

His plea must have touched the right chord, for the housemother nodded. "All right, but you cannot come inside."

"I understand." Mrs. Weld closed the door, as if to emphasize her decree. While he waited for her to return, Brad leaned against the building and glanced both ways. As was normal for this time of the night, Main Street was deserted. Shopkeepers had long since boarded their windows, and mill workers were inside, preparing for the next day.

Idly, Brad noticed the evidence that a horse had passed by recently. Very recently. The equine calling card had not been there an hour ago when he'd escorted Eleanor back to her boardinghouse. Brad wrinkled his nose. Though some might decry Mr. Ford's invention, a Model T left no aromatic reminders of its presence. Judging from the pile in the street, the horse had been stopped, not merely passing through. Brad raised an eyebrow, wondering who had brought a horse here. This section of Main rarely saw anything other than pedestrian traffic, and Sunday evening was an odd time for visitors. A memory tugged at the back of Brad's mind. Father had mentioned a man renting a horse and carriage to explore the countryside. Had he gotten lost and somehow found himself on this part of Main?

Brad's speculation ceased as the boardinghouse door opened. He turned, eager to see the woman who had promised to be his bride. Instead, he faced the housemother, her forehead lined with concern. "I don't understand," Mrs. Weld said. It was a measure of her distress that she left the house and placed a hand on Brad's arm. "Eleanor is not here. Deborah and Virginia thought she was in their room, but she's not. She's not downstairs either. I don't understand," the housemother repeated. "It's not like Eleanor to leave without telling someone."

Brad had heard of the hairs on the back of one's neck rising. If he'd thought about the phrase at all, he had imagined it to be a figure of speech. It was not. He felt his hairs rise as fear flooded his veins. Though he prayed he was mistaken, his instincts shouted that something was desperately wrong. First it appeared

Eleanor had told no one about their engagement, and now she was missing. That was not like her. She might have had a reason for not sharing the news—although Brad could not imagine what it could be—but she would have done nothing to cause others to worry. That included leaving the boardinghouse without telling someone where she was going.

"There must be a logical explanation," Brad said, amazed at how calm his voice sounded, while his thoughts were tumbling faster than rose petals in a storm. "She must be close by." It was the only reason he could conjure. If she stepped outside for fresh air, there would have been no need to tell anyone. That must be what had happened. Eleanor had been here an hour ago. Mrs. Weld confirmed that. She also confirmed that Eleanor's hat was still inside. Brad nodded when he heard that, for everything confirmed his thoughts. Like his mother, Eleanor was a stickler for propriety. She would not have gone for a walk without her hat. That meant she must be close at hand, somewhere where she would not be observed. Perhaps she was resting and had fallen asleep. That must be it. A simple, innocent explanation.

"I'll find her," he announced confidently.

Brad rounded the corner of the boardinghouse. If Eleanor were resting anywhere, it would be here, in the place where he'd spotted her and Deborah sitting on the grass, trying desperately to hide their bare feet. Surely she was here. She was not. His spirits plummeted at the sight of the empty lawn. Unwilling to believe he'd been mistaken, Brad looked around again, searching for a trace of Eleanor. His eyes narrowed when he spotted a section of grass that appeared to be matted. His heart racing as fast as his feet, Brad ran to the spot, only to feel his hopes sink even lower, for the grass looked as if it had been trampled by feet, not by someone sitting on it. Eleanor would have sat, not ran around in circles. He turned, determined not to let discouragement overcome him. He would find her. He had to.

Brad took a deep breath as he tried to decide where to search next. *Oh, Eleanor, where have you gone?* He looked across the street at his boardinghouse. Would she have come to see him? She'd never done that, but then, she'd never before promised to marry him. He'd ask Mrs. Larimer if he'd had any visitors.

As Brad turned, glancing at the grass one more time, he glimpsed a speck of white. Odd. It wasn't a flower petal or a bird feather. The wind would have blown those away. Curious, he plucked it from the ground, then frowned as he recognized it. *Be careful what you ask for.* The adage reverberated in his mind. He'd wanted proof Eleanor had been here, and he'd gotten it. Unfortunately, he'd gotten more than that. He stared at the object now carefully nestled in his palm. There was no doubt of its identity. It was a piece of shell, not an ordinary shell, but part of Eleanor's necklace.

As fear clutched his heart, squeezing it so tightly he thought it might break, Brad tried to find a logical, innocent explanation. There were none. The shells were sturdy. They would not have broken under normal wear.

Brad's heart contracted further as the matted grass took on a sinister appearance. Had the matting been caused by a struggle? It was unthinkable, and yet he could find no other reason that would also explain the broken necklace.

Brad looked up and down the street, hoping against hope that Eleanor would suddenly appear. She did not. Main Street was empty, save for the horse's calling card. *The horse*. Brad grimaced as his fears coalesced. Eleanor had left on the horse or, more likely, in a carriage the horse had pulled. The shell fragment said she had not left of her own volition. Anger threatened to overwhelm Brad's fears as he faced the realization that Eleanor had been abducted. Sweet, wonderful Eleanor, the woman he loved, was gone.

It wasn't difficult to imagine who was responsible. Hidden Falls was a quiet, peaceful town. She had no enemies here. Thank goodness she had told him about her uncle and his determination to marry her to a suitor of his choosing. If she hadn't, Brad might have spent precious hours trying to puzzle out a reason for her disappearance. Now it all made sense, especially coupled with what Father had said. The stranger who'd come to town on today's train and had rented a horse and carriage was either Eleanor's uncle or the despicable Mr. Warren. It wasn't coincidence that a stranger had arrived the very day Eleanor disappeared. Somehow those men had learned where she was, and one of them had abducted her.

As adrenaline rushed through Brad's veins, his

thoughts began to coalesce. There was only one thing to do. He would find Eleanor. Thank goodness he had a motor car. His Model T would outrun any horse. He frowned as he realized speed wasn't a problem. Direction was. Without a trail, he could be driving in the opposite direction. Though his imagination conjured pictures of what Eleanor's abductor would do when he got her to their destination, Brad pushed them aside. Speculation was futile; it only distracted him from his mission: finding Eleanor.

There had to be a way. If they'd had recent rain, he could follow the carriage tracks, but the ground was hard-packed. Still, he looked in both directions, searching for a rut, another horse deposit, anything. And then he saw it. In the distance, something gleamed white. Brad was out of breath when he reached it, but elation filled him as he recognized the shell. She was incredible. His Eleanor was the most wonderful woman on earth. She'd left him a trail.

It seemed as though it had been an eternity, though her watch declared that only twenty-seven minutes had passed. Eleanor frowned as she looked at what had once been her necklace. Only four shells remained. She'd been doling them out carefully, dropping one every minute. She tried not to think of what would happen if she ran out of shells before they arrived. How would Brad—how would anyone—find her if the trail ended?

She stared out the window, searching for landmarks. The countryside reminded her of the day she and Brad had picked peaches. That day she'd been with the man she loved, her heart filled with anticipation. Today she was with a man she despised, a man who was taking her somewhere, but not, it seemed, back to New York. The sun remained on the left side of the carriage, its position telling her they were heading north.

How many miles had they traveled in twenty-seven minutes? How long would it be before anyone knew she was gone? As soon as Virginia and Deborah saw the empty room, they'd realize something was amiss, but that would happen only when they retired for the evening, and that was not for another—Eleanor consulted her watch again—thirty-three minutes. By then the sun would have set, darkness hiding the clues she had so carefully sown along the route.

Eleanor pressed her lips together. She wouldn't think about darkness, for if she did, the despair she had been holding at bay would rush in. That must not happen. If she had any chance of foiling Mr. Warren's plans, she needed to keep her wits about her. Cunning and surprise, Virginia had told her, were her most powerful weapons.

Eleanor felt the carriage slow, then lurch as it turned off the main road onto a rutted lane. Quickly, she hurled the remaining shells out the window, hoping they'd land close enough to the road to be visible. They'd mean nothing to anyone except Brad, but Eleanor had to believe that would be enough.

She looked down the lane, hoping for the sight of something reassuring, something that would quiet the pounding of her heart. A simple whitewashed farmhouse stood at the end. Her spirits rose. At least this was not Clifford Warren's house. He had boasted that he owned a redbrick mansion. Though Eleanor had doubted the mansion part of his tale, he had struck her as a man of limited imagination, and so she had believed his home was redbrick. The only stonework on this house was a fieldstone chimney. The few scraggly flowers struggling for survival near the front porch told Eleanor that if a woman lived here, she possessed limited gardening skills.

The carriage lurched again as Mr. Warren brought it to a stop. "Get out," he ordered as he unlatched the door. "And don't try any trickery. It won't work. The parson knows all about you."

The parson? A chill of pure fear snaked its way down Eleanor's spine as the last piece fit into the puzzle. Mr. Warren planned to marry her. Today. She should have realized that was why he'd come to Hidden Falls, why he'd abducted her, and why he'd brought her to this remote farmhouse. Though his speech had made her believe he might be a little touched in the head, he wasn't. Instead, he was a coldly calculating man, determined to have his heart's desire: her inheritance.

"You can't marry me without my consent," Eleanor said, hoping her voice did not betray her fears. She looked around desperately, searching for a way to escape. There was none. Her earlier attempt had shown her the futility of trying to outrun Mr. Warren.

As if he'd read her thoughts, he wrapped his arm around her waist and tugged her close to him. "You think I can't marry you." His smile sent another frisson down Eleanor's spine. "That's where you're wrong, Missy. Money can buy almost anything, including a parson. He's prepared to testify you came here of your own volition."

This man was evil. She couldn't—she wouldn't—marry him. Eleanor thought quickly. Marriage involved more than vows. There were also documents.

"I won't sign anything."

This time he laughed, a sound even more chilling than his smile. "How could you, with a broken hand?"

"I don't have . . ." Eleanor's smile faded as she admitted the truth. This was all part of a plan, a carefully concocted plan that left nothing to chance. Uncle Abel must have designed it, for Eleanor doubted Mr. Warren was clever enough to account for all the possibilities. The man who believed himself to be her future bridegroom was strong and determined, but he was not overly blessed with intelligence. There had to be a way she could outsmart him.

As they made their way to the house, Mr. Warren's arm wrapped so firmly around her waist that Eleanor knew she had no chance of escape, the front door opened and a tall man wearing a Roman collar emerged.

"Are you Clifford Warren?" At the affirmative nod, the parson continued, "It's about time you got here. C'mon in."

He ushered them into a small parlor. Though clean, the interior of the house betrayed the absence of a feminine influence. The lace curtains had yellowed with age, and the horsehair settee was faded. No crocheted doilies, antimacassars, or ornaments of any kind softened the room's austerity.

The man wasted no time. As soon as they were inside, he opened a thick book and began to read, "Dearly beloved, forasmuch as marriage is a holy estate . . ."

Eleanor had heard those words dozens of times before. She'd dreamed of the day she would hear them pronounced for her. But never once had she dreamed that she would be standing here in a parson's parlor, being married against her will to a man as despicable as Mr. Warren.

"I won't agree to this."

"Shut your mouth." Mr. Warren punctuated his words with a jab to Eleanor's ribs.

"I won't," she repeated, refusing to be cowed. Instead of facing the minister, as any bride-to-be would, she turned and glared at the man determined to become her bridegroom. "How do you know he's a real minister?" she demanded. Perhaps if she created confusion, she could delay the ceremony. Until it was fully dark, she wouldn't abandon hope that someone had discovered her absence and was looking for her.

"You won't get any of my money unless the marriage is valid," she said firmly. The parson ceased his recitation and stared at her. This was, Eleanor was willing to bet, one of the most unusual wedding ceremonies he'd performed. "My lawyer and banker will see to that. I'll ensure that they do."

Mr. Warren's lips twisted in a snarl. "You won't be

doing much of anything, Missy. Once the honeymoon is over, you are going to suffer an unfortunate accident." The chuckle accompanying his words left no doubt the accident would be fatal.

Eleanor's brain refused to consider the possibility of her impending death. She couldn't die, not before she and Brad had a chance to marry and create their own happily-ever-after. Eleanor gave the parson a beseeching look. Surely the man had some innate decency.

For a moment there was no sound save the horse's neighing and a cricket's chirp. Then for the first time since she'd interrupted him, the parson spoke. "Wait one minute. I cannot be party to murder. The Good Book says 'thou shalt not kill.' "

"So you do have a conscience." Eleanor nodded with satisfaction. "Let's stop this farce of a wedding right now."

She saw hesitation in the parson's eyes. As he started to close his book, Mr. Warren clapped his hand over Eleanor's mouth. "Cease this chatter, both of you." He glared at the parson. "What happens later is none of your business. You're being paid plenty to marry us. Do it!"

The man's eyes widened for a second before he lowered them to his hymnal. "Into this holy estate this man and woman come now to be united." As the parson intoned the familiar words, Mr. Warren dropped the hand that covered Eleanor's mouth, preferring, it appeared, to grasp her waist with both hands. "If anyone, therefore, can show just cause why they may not be lawfully joined together, let him now speak, or else forever hold his peace."

There were reasons, many of them, why this marriage should not occur. "I do not wish to marry this man," Eleanor said, citing the most important of them. "You heard him. The only reason he wants to marry me is my money."

But that, it appeared, created no impediment for the parson. He frowned at Eleanor, then turned his attention back to his book.

Eleanor swallowed deeply. She wouldn't agree; she wouldn't sign the marriage certificate, but that might not be enough. Even against her will, it appeared she would soon be Mrs. Clifford Warren. Through the open window, she heard the horse whinny, and then she heard another sound, the one she'd been praying for. She kept her face impassive, hoping neither man understood the significance of the mechanical rattle.

"Clifford Warren, wilt thou have this woman . . ."

Before the parson could finish asking whether Mr. Warren would honor and keep Eleanor in sickness and health, he said, "I will."

The noise had stopped. Nodding at Mr. Warren, the parson continued. "Eleanor Menger, wilt thou . . ."

Heavy footsteps pounded the front porch, and the door was flung open. "She will not."

Eleanor turned and smiled at the man she loved. He'd found her! He'd said he wanted to be a knight in shining armor, rescuing her. Brad's wishes had come true.

"Who are you?" the parson demanded.

"I'm the man she's going to marry." His voice firm, Brad took another step into the room. "Let Eleanor go," he ordered when he saw that Clifford Warren held her.

In response, Mr. Warren tightened his grip, pulling Eleanor closer to him. Though only one arm was wrapped around her, it felt as strong as steel. "She's mine," he announced. "You'll never have her."

Brad took another step forward, his hands fisted, his stance telegraphing his willingness to fight.

Mr. Warren's laugh bore no mirth. "You won't win." His chuckle sent a shiver of dread along Eleanor's spine.

"No?" Eleanor could practically feel Brad measuring the distance, trying to determine how he could tackle Mr. Warren without hurting her.

"No." The man who held her laughed again. Before Brad could react, he reached into his coat and pulled out a gun.

Eleanor gasped. Behind her, she heard the parson whimper. He would provide no help. The weapon was large and ugly and, at this range, even a poor marksman could hardly fail to inflict a serious wound . . . or worse.

"Leave or I'll use this." His voice nothing short of a gloat, Mr. Warren cocked the trigger and pointed the gun at Brad.

He would use it. Eleanor had not a doubt of that. The man had already planned to kill her. One more death would not trouble his conscience. She couldn't let him do that. Brad's life was too precious to be sacrificed.

Eleanor looked at the man of her dreams. Though he'd not taken another step forward, he hadn't turned to leave. He wouldn't. She could read that in the set of his shoulders and in the fire blazing in his eyes. Brad was like those medieval knights he admired. He had come to save his lady's honor, and nothing would stop him. He would rescue Eleanor, even if it cost him his life.

At one time, Eleanor had thought the troubadours' tales romantic. But that was before she was faced with the reality of seeing the man she loved injured or worse. There was nothing at all romantic about that.

Cunning, Eleanor reminded herself. There had to be a way to force Mr. Warren to drop the gun. He was in the wrong position for her to stomp on his foot again. Apparently he had learned from that experience, for he'd been careful to keep her boots out of range of his appendages. What else had Deborah taught her? Eleanor took a quick breath, remembering their second lesson. Maybe, just maybe, that would work.

"Go away, Brad," she said, hoping to keep Mr. Warren's attention focused on him. "I'm sorry you drove all this way for naught." She kept her voice even as she shifted her body ever so slightly. The correct position, Virginia had emphasized, was critical. "Go home, Brad." Another shift. "There's nothing you can do." Now! As she pronounced the final word, Eleanor jabbed her elbow into Mr. Warren's stomach.

"Ow!" The cry was feral in its intensity. Eleanor didn't care, for as he clutched his stomach, Mr. Warren dropped the gun and loosened his grip on her. The second's reprieve was what she needed. She jerked free and ran, kicking the weapon into the corner of the room.

At the same instant, Brad leaped forward and knocked Mr. Warren to the floor. The man landed with a satisfying thud and another primal scream. Without the gun, Mr. Warren had no chance. Brad was younger, stronger, more determined. The older man surrendered without a struggle.

Brad turned Eleanor's kidnapper onto his face and yanked his arms behind his back. "Find me something to tie him up." He directed his words to the parson.

The man was clearly appalled. "This is a house of peace."

Eleanor almost laughed at the absurdity of the words. Brad, however, was in no laughing mood. "You should have considered that when you agreed to his scheme. Now, are you going to help me or will I have to report you to the sheriff for abetting a criminal?" The threat accomplished its goal, and a moment later, the parson returned with two sturdy belts.

"Do you want to help?" Brad asked. Eleanor did indeed.

"You'll pay for this, Missy," Mr. Warren snarled. "If it's the last thing I do, you'll pay for it."

Brad tightened the belt around his captive's wrists. "If you so much as approach Eleanor," he said, his voice low and fierce, "I can promise you it *will* be the last thing you do."

Mr. Warren made no reply.

Brad rose and extended his hand to Eleanor. "All

right, parson. It seems to me you were paid to perform a marriage ceremony. Let's continue."

He smiled at Eleanor. "Are you ready?" She nodded.

"But . . ." The parson began to stutter.

"Start over. There's a new bridegroom."

Epilogue

*O*ne month later

"It's so romantic." Virginia sighed as she adjusted Eleanor's veil. "Your wedding is all anyone in Hidden Falls can talk about."

Deborah sniffed the bouquet of roses she was holding for Eleanor. "It's the first time a mill worker was married in this church."

Eleanor smiled, pleased that, despite the revelation of her background, the majority of Hidden Falls still viewed her as a mill worker. There'd been an outcry over Clifford Warren's abduction of her, with some of the townspeople calling for a hanging. Eleanor proposed a more painful—and appropriate—punishment. Since it was a desire for money that had driven Mr. Warren to his actions, she claimed the most fitting penalty was a hefty fine. Thanks to Clifford Warren's greed, the lyceum would be funded for the next five years.

Today Eleanor and her two closest friends stood in the small room off the vestibule, waiting for the last of the guests to be seated. Eleanor smiled again. "It's probably the first time anyone in Hidden Falls—mill worker or not—was married to the same person for the second time."

Though the parson had completed the ceremony and produced what he claimed was a legal marriage certificate, she and Brad hadn't been convinced the ceremony was legal, and so they'd decided to have a second wedding—what Mrs. Harrod persisted in referring to as a "real" wedding.

To everyone's surprise, Eleanor had remained in the boardinghouse, although she had left the mill. Her future mother-in-law had insisted Eleanor had no time to work, pointing out that this was her only chance to plan a wedding, and she wanted it done right. "Right" had turned out to be a ceremony as elaborate as any Eleanor's own mother might have planned.

Accompanied by Brad and both of his parents, Eleanor had gone to New York, meeting first with her attorney, then her banker. Only then had she returned to the house where she'd spent the last eight years.

"Uncle Abel," she had said when he'd ushered the four of them into his parlor, "I'd like you to meet my husband." Though she suspected that Clifford Warren had delivered the news of their failed scheme, she wanted to be certain there was no misunderstanding.

The man had sputtered, shouting obscenities when he realized his source of income had ended. "You'll regret this," he screamed as she rose to leave.

"No, I won't," Eleanor had replied with a sweet smile. "Not until the Hudson River flows north."

That had been four weeks ago, four weeks filled with fittings for her wedding gown and endless consultations with Mrs. Harrod about the flower colors, the church decorations, the food for the reception. Now at last the preparations were complete. Today was Eleanor's wedding day.

As the music changed, she took the bouquet from Deborah and opened the door to the sanctuary. It was time for the sisters to walk down the aisle. Though Eleanor had feared her future mother-in-law might object to having mill workers in the wedding party, Mrs. Harrod had nodded her approval when Eleanor had explained her choice of attendants. "Of course, my dear," she had said. "We must find them the perfect dresses."

"Don't forget to smile," Eleanor admonished the two perfectly dressed sisters. They flashed her broad grins before tempering them into radiant smiles.

"Are you ready?" Mr. Harrod asked a minute later. He had seemed oddly pleased when Eleanor had asked if he would take her father's place and escort her down the aisle.

"Oh, yes." She was ready, more than ready. This was the day she had dreamed of since she was a child, the day when dreams would become reality, when she would become a bride, a wife, and maybe one day a mother. And so, though she was tempted to run, Eleanor walked slowly and sedately down the aisle, her smile growing as each step brought her closer to the man she loved, the man who was her knight in shining armor, the man who brought joy and laughter to each day, the man who had embroidered the ordinary fabric of her life with the golden thread of love. Brad.

Author's Letter

Dear Reader,

Just one more, please. If I had a dollar for each time I've said that, I'd be a wealthy woman. It started when I was a child and my parents would read me bedtime stories. They were supposed to lull me to sleep, but they had the opposite effect, for I never wanted those stories to end. Once I could read on my own, the refrain became *one more chapter* and then *one more book.* I'd fall in love with the characters and didn't want to let them go. That's why I've always enjoyed series books. They give me the opportunity to revisit familiar places and meet old friends for the second and third time.

Now that I'm an author, I have the pleasure of creating my own stories and, yes, many of them are part of a series. *The Golden Thread* is the fifth Hidden Falls Romance, with at least two more to come. Were you intrigued by the references to Jane and Anne Moreland's love stories? If so, I urge you to read *Painted Ponies* (Anne's story) and *The Brass Ring* (Jane's). And if the Sempert sisters caught your fancy, you'll be glad to know that Virginia and Deborah have their own books.

While Deborah has had beaux galore and is betrothed to one of the farmers near home, Virginia's favorite companions are books. That's why she's saving the money she earns at Moreland Mills, not for her dowry, but so she can attend normal school and become a teacher. Marriage and children, Virginia is certain, are not in her future. All that changes the day Anthony Borman comes to Hidden Falls. Curious? I hope so. *The Silver Loom,* Virginia and Anthony's story, will be available in early 2009.

In the meantime, may I recommend my War Brides trilogy to you? *Dancing in the Rain, Whistling in the Dark,* and *Laughing at the Thunder* tell the stories of three sisters caught up in the War to End All Wars. They've received excellent reviews, and *Dancing in the Rain* was even nominated for an award.

As pleased as I am by reviewers' comments, what I love most is hearing from readers. Don't be shy. Please let me know what you've enjoyed about my books and what you'd like to see next. I've said it before, but it bears repeating: you're the reason I write.

Happy reading!
Amanda Harte